The Big Book of Things that Go Bump in the Night

Ghost stories around the U.S.

Jannette Quackenbush

Copyright © 2025 by Jannette Quackenbush

ISBN-13: 978-1-940087-71-9

21 Crows Dusk to Dawn Publishing, 21 Crows, LLC All rights reserved. No part of this book may be reproduced or transmitted in any form or by any means, electronic or mechanical, including photocopying, recording, or by any information storage and retrieval system, without permission in writing from the copyright owner. This is a work of fiction. Names, characters, places, and incidents either are the product of the author's imagination or are used fictitiously, and any resemblance to any actual persons, living or dead, events, or locales is entirely coincidental. This book was printed in the United States of America.

"From ghoulies and ghosties and long-leggedy beasties and things that go bump in the night, Good Lord deliver us."
An old prayer by an unknown author

ALABAMA: A GRUESOME TRUTH GROWS FROM THE GRAVE—BOYINGTON OAK	6
ALABAMA: OWL HOLLOW—ABEL'S LIGHT	9
ALASKA: THE REVENANT OF PORT CHATHAM	13
ALASKA: THE HAUNTING OF SOAPY SMITH'S SALOON	17
ARIZONA: BLOODIEST CABIN IN ARIZONA	21
ARIZONA: SOMETHING WATCHES IN CANYON DIABLO	25
ARKANSAS: DEAD BRIDE OF THE RIVER	29
ARKANSAS: A GHOST THAT WON'T DIE	32
CALIFORNIA: WINEVILLE CHICKEN FARM MURDERS—SOME ARE STILL THERE	36
CALIFORNIA: PRESTON CASTLE—THE BLOOD IN THE BRICKS	40
COLORADO: THE THING THAT WENT BUMP IN THE NIGHT	45
COLORADO: THE DEAD RISE IN LUDLOW	50
CONNECTICUT: THE REEF TAKES AT PENFIELD LIGHTHOUSE	54
DELAWARE: TO MOST IT WAS JUST A CROOKED ROAD...WITH A GHOST	58
FLORIDA: HAUNTING END OF ED "BLOODY" WATSON	62
FLORIDA: THE HAUNTING OF ST. AUGUSTINE LIGHTHOUSE	67
GEORGIA: THE DEAD STILL DEFEND FORT MCALLISTER	71
GEORGIA: BREAKFAST IN HELL—THE HAUNTING OF OLD NUMBER 7	75
HAWAII: KASHA AT THE KAIMUKI HOUSE	79
HAWAII: DEAD CURVE—WHERE URBAN LEGEND AND TRUE HORROR MEET	83
IDAHO: CRYBABY RIVER	87
IDAHO: LADY BLUEBEARD—BLACK WIDOW WHO WOULDN'T STAY DEAD	90
ILLINOIS: BLOODY GULCH MURDER	93
ILLINOIS: OLD BOOK AND THE CRYING TREE—PEORIA STATE HOSPITAL	96
INDIANA: BIG TUNNEL—THE DANCING DEAD LIGHT	99
INDIANA: THE DARK WEEPER IN THE WOODS—STEPP CEMETERY	103
IOWA: THE BLACK ANGEL OF OAKLAND CEMETERY	107
IOWA: THE HOLLOW WHERE PEARL WAITS—THE MOSSY GLEN MURDERS	111
KANSAS: DEAD MAN IN THE HOLLOW—THE LOST NAME OF MALLOW	115
KANSAS: BLUE LIGHT LADY—FORT HAYS	119
KENTUCKY: HEADLESS HORROR OF FORT THOMAS	123
KENTUCKY: GHOST DOG WITH A BONE TO PICK	127
LOUISIANA: THE STORM JULIA SANG—FRENIER LOUISIANA	131
LOUISIANA: MOANING MONA LISA SMILES—CITY PARK, NEW ORLEANS	135
MAINE: THE DEVIL'S FOOTPRINT—NORTH MANCHESTER MEETING HOUSE	139
MAINE: DARK SHADOWS ON WOOD ISLAND	142
MARYLAND: UNSETTLED SOULS AT WISE'S WELL	146
MARYLAND: STICKPILE TUNNEL—GREEN RIDGE FOREST	150
MASSACHUSETTS: PALE GHOST OF BOSTON COMMON	153
MICHIGAN: PAULDING GHOST LIGHT	157
MICHIGAN: THE DROWNED GIRL—BECKONING MINNIE	160
MINNESOTA: BOBBING LANTERN OF ARCOLA HIGH BRIDGE	164
MISSISSIPPI: OLD MAN STUCKEY'S REMAINS	167
MISSISSIPPI: THE ANGEL THAT WATCHES THE DEAD . . . AND THE LIVING	170
MISSOURI: THE HAUNTING OF BLOODY HILL	173

MONTANA: SISTER IRENE WILL NOT REST IN VIRGINIA CITY	176
NEBRASKA: DON'T LOOK TOO LONG IN THE PLATTE RIVER	179
NEBRASKA: THE BLOOD THAT SOAKED SEVEN SISTERS ROAD	181
NEVADA: THE MYSTERIOUS WOMAN IN WHITE OF VIRGINIA CITY	185
NEW HAMPSHIRE: THE STAIRCASE TO NOWHERE IN THE WOODS	187
NEW HAMPSHIRE: THE PALE SENTINEL OF WHITE ISLAND	190
NEW JERSEY: THE DEAD BOY BENEATH THE BRIDGE ON CLINTON ROAD	193
NEW MEXICO: MYSTERIOUS CEMETERY LIGHTS IN DAWSON	195
NEW YORK: THE WEEPING WIDOW OF AMSTERDAM	198
NEW YORK: THE RESTLESS BENEATH: WASHINGTON SQUARE PARK	201
NORTH CAROLINA: THE TAR RIVER BANSHEE	204
NORTH CAROLINA: LOST COVE—WHERE GHOSTS LINGER	207
NORTH DAKOTA: RIVERSIDE CEMETERY—KNOCK-KNOCK GHOST	211
OHIO: FEU-FOLLET—TINY LIGHTS BECKON AT GOLL WOODS	213
OHIO: THE MOONVILLE BRAKEMAN—THE RAILS REMEMBER THE DEAD	216
OKLAHOMA: DEAD WOMAN CROSSING—A BRIDGE CRIES OUT	220
OREGON: THE GRAY LADY OF HECETA HEAD OREGON COAST	224
PENNSYLVANIA: THE BULLET THAT FOUND JENNIE WADE—GETTYSBURG	227
RHODE ISLAND: WHERE POE KNOCKED AND NEVER LEFT	230
SOUTH CAROLINA: MURRELLS INLET– WHERE LOVE ROTS IN THE MARSH	233
SOUTH DAKOTA: BROKEN BOOT GOLD MINE—THE DEAD ARE NOT SO DEAD	236
TENNESSEE: THE GHOST OF ROARING FORKS, GREAT SMOKY MOUNTAINS	240
TENNESSEE: THE BELL WITCH—WHERE THE DEVIL CAME TO VISIT	244
TEXAS: THE HOLLOW THAT WON'T LET GO	248
TEXAS: GHOST ROAD	251
UTAH: WHITE LADY OF SPRING CANYON	254
VERMONT: THE GRAVE WITH A WINDOW	257
VERMONT: THE DEVIL'S FOOTPRINTS OF GLASTENBURY MOUNTAIN	258
VIRGINIA: SARVER SHELTER	261
VIRGINIA: BUNNY MAN OF COLCHESTER OVERPASS	262
WASHINGTON: FORT VANCOUVER GRAY LADY	264
WEST VIRGINIA: LAKE SHAWNEE AMUSEMENT PARK	267
WEST VIRGINA: BOOGER HOLE	270
WISCONSIN: BEAST OF BRAY ROAD	273
WISCONSIN: THE RIDGEWAY GHOST	276
WYOMING: POLLY BARTLETT: MURDERESS OF SLAUGHTERHOUSE GULCH	280
CITATIONS	284

Alabama: A Gruesome Truth Grows from the Grave—Boyington Oak

A Lifeless Body is Found

On a gloomy May morning, as a heavy mist clung low to the earth like a shroud, the mutilated body of young Nathaniel Frost was discovered behind the old city cemetery in Mobile, Alabama. His lifeless corpse was crumpled in the weeds, stabbed brutally—wounds torn across his back, head, chest, and hands. It was a gruesome, chilling scene.

Authorities were summoned quickly, but by then, the air itself already seemed to know something unspoken and vile.

A Villain Was Chosen

Witnesses reported seeing Frost walking the cemetery path the evening before, accompanied by a friend, a fellow known well in town—Charles Boyington, a 21-year-old printer who had recently arrived from Connecticut. Boyington had charm, a quick wit, and a fondness for music and parties.

But he also gambled.

And he came from the North—outsider blood. He'd rented a room with Nathaniel Frost, a sickly boy with lungs rotted by consumption, whom Boyington had taken under his wing. They were inseparable—seen often in the nearby graveyard reading aloud the poetic epitaphs on the headstones, picking wild berries among the graves. But in a town eager for a villain, friendship meant nothing. The whispers turned fast.

Frost, it was said, owed Boyington money.

That was motive enough. When Boyington left town shortly after the murder—boarding a riverboat, chasing fortune at cards—the noose began to tighten. Officers tracked him to a stop downriver and hauled him back, his protests of innocence falling on deaf ears.

A Curse

The trial that followed was a spectacle of failure: shoddy evidence, a disinterested jury, and a defense barely worth the name. Boyington was found guilty in a swift, merciless fashion.

On February 20, 1835, he stood before the court and, with eyes burning not with fear but fury, proclaimed a curse: "From my grave, an oak will rise. It will stand as proof of my innocence and a judgment on those who condemned me."

He was hanged and buried in the Church Street Graveyard… and in time, the earth stirred.

A Tree Grew

A single oak tree grew from that lonely grave—twisting upward through stone and soil, defiant and strong. Locals say it sprang from Boyington's very heart, unbowed and unbroken even in death. *The Boyington Oak*, they call it. And still, it stands, roots sunk deep into the ground where injustice once walked in broad daylight.

Its branches whisper in the wind—of betrayal, of truth buried and clawing to be heard, and of men who damned a boy to die while the real evil went on in silence. That tree is not just a legend. It is a verdict from beyond the veil. A living sentence against those who think their sins will stay hidden.

Because some truths will rise. And some ghosts will not rest.

In 1847, many years after Charles Boyington's hanging, the landlord of the two young men confessed to the murder of Frost on his deathbed.

Alabama: Owl Hollow—Abel's Light

Owl Hollow is a deep, brooding ravine nestled between the looming shadows of Lookout Mountain and Shinbone Ridge, buried in the dark woods of northeastern Alabama. It's a place where daylight feels reluctant to enter, and the wind moves through the trees like it's carrying secrets. Roughly five miles northeast of Turkeytown—the ancient homeland of Chief Little Turkey—the hollow sits in a quiet pocket of forgotten land near the Coosa River, where the earth is fertile, the woods are thick, and neighbors are few.

The Vanishing

In the early 1900s, the Abel family—a man, his wife, and their three children—built a modest homestead in the hollow's heart. Among them was four-year-old Henry Abel, a wide-eyed boy with a laugh that echoed off the trees like birdsong.

But one bitter December night, when frost clung to every branch and the wind howled through the ridge like a warning, Henry vanished.

At first, the family searched desperately through the underbrush and trails around their home, calling his name into the trees. When that yielded nothing, the alarm spread to neighbors, and soon, the whole community was combing the woods.

Lanterns swung low across the forest floor, dogs barked into the dark, and prayers were whispered between clenched teeth. But days passed. Then weeks.

And the snow fell harder.

There was No Sign of Henry.

The neighbors gave up one by one, returning to the comfort of their own fires. But Henry's father could not let go. He became obsessed and desperate.

Something inside him had snapped.

Every morning before dawn, he saddled his horse, lifted a kerosene lantern, and rode out into the growing dark, calling his son's name to the trees—always returning long after dark, empty and hollow-eyed.

Until one night…

He didn't come home.

His wife found his horse standing alone in the barn, panting, sweaty, jittery, and dragging reins in the dirt. It was near dusk the next day when Henry's elder brother stumbled upon a terrible sight:

His father's lifeless body dangling from a forked branch of a gnarled and ancient Blackjack Oak.

He was caught by the neck where the trail dipped low.

The man still clutched the lantern in his rigid dead hand—its glass cracked, the flame still burning—his eyes staring wide into nothing. They buried him quietly. The woods fell silent again.

But then... the Light Returned.

Not in the barn. Not in any living hand. But moving slowly through Owl Hollow—a dim, flickering glow, weaving between trees as if still held high by a rider searching endlessly for his lost child. It appears only in the dead of winter when the leaves have fallen, and the sky hangs low and gray—from mid-December to March before the spring's growth swallows the view once more.

Locals say that if you see the light, do not follow it.

They say it is seeking help to find little Henry, but it will lead you astray, winding you deeper into the woods until the air grows thin and strange. Until you lose the trail. Until you get lost, too.

Because you can keep searching—outside the bounds of the spirit world, where the dead are tethered, and the living still have feet to wander. You can go farther. Far enough that the lantern fades, all left is the whisper of wind through skeletal trees.

And that's when you vanish. Like Henry.

Or perish. Like his father. And then, the light returns, hungry, flickering, looking for another who can go even farther than you.

Because perhaps it isn't the search for the little boy at all.

Perhaps it never was.

Perhaps it's an ancient curse buried in that hollow long before the Abels came. Something older than settlers. Older than names. It doesn't want a resolution. It wants repetition.

A cycle. A loop. A hollow in more ways than one.

And if you listen closely—just beneath the rustling of the dead leaves, just after the wind dies down—you might still hear a father's voice, cracked and hollow:

"Come. Come. Help me find Henry."

He wants someone who can search beyond the veil with the same obsession he felt and not care if you die too—or pass on the weight of something darker—he will never let you go.

Alaska: The Revenant of Port Chatham

Something Ancient Roams

In the early 20th century, Portlock—tucked away in the misty cradle of Port Chatham Bay—was a thriving fish cannery village built by a tight-knit community of Aleut and Russian settlers. But long before it became a town, the land carried a warning. The local Native people had already turned their backs on it, refusing to live or even work there.

They spoke of something ancient that roamed the forests, something they called Nantinaq.

Nantinaq

Towering, covered in hair, and more than just flesh and bone, Nantinaq was no mere animal. It was a presence—part spirit, part beast—supernatural, with a hunger for solitude and a hatred for trespassers. Those who entered its domain had a way of vanishing. Some were never seen again. Others were found broken and bloodied as if torn apart by something far more powerful than any bear.

Still, the cannery thrived. The sea was rich, and the isolation—surrounded by rainforest and hemmed in by cliffs—kept outsiders away. For a time, it was quiet. Peaceful, even. Then, the forest stirred again.

The Vanishings *Again*

The disappearances returned, sudden and merciless, as if the land had remembered its curse. And with it came whispers, old fears reborn. Like a revenant, the creature returned—Nantinaq, the shadow in the trees, the thing that walks between this world and whatever waits beyond it.

One by one, men heading out for hunting or trapping expeditions disappeared into the woods, their bodies later found torn apart in a way no bear or known predator could do. Limbs were shredded, and bones snapped like twigs. Or no corpse was found at all. Those who left in boats from the bay would not return, and their vessels were found rusted and abandoned on the beach.

People saw a massive, shadowy creature lurking in the woods. The older locals whispered that it could get no worse: Nantinaq had come back.

In 1940, a man named Andrew Kamluck was found dead in the woods, his head crushed by a piece of logging equipment. There was no sign of a struggle, no footprints, and no explanation for his death.

Another trapper vanished, and his dogs returned days later—bloody, terrified, and dragging a broken sled. To ensure safety, men established lookout rotations at night, children were kept indoors, and hunters refused to go alone.

The U.S. government and some military personnel were reportedly aware of the area. They did not formally investigate the mysterious events surrounding it.

By 1949, after the construction of Alaska Route 1 and the series of vanishings, the remaining families had enough. They packed their belongings, boarded boats, and left Portlock for good. The post office shut down, and the cannery fell silent. Whatever had claimed the missing individuals and the town itself also began to reclaim the village.

"It's wearing my face."

A legend was passed along in 1973. A logging crew was sent to survey the area. One night, a worker named Bill Haskins vanished. His radio crackled with heavy breathing before going dead. They found him days later near a waterfall—his face frozen in terror, eyes wide open, his hands shredded like he'd tried to claw through solid rock.

Locals say his ghost wanders the old cannery, repeating the exact words over the radio frequency he last used: "It's wearing my face."

Screams in the Wind

Tourists who try to camp there report hearing screaming from the woods, dragging chains, and once—most chillingly—someone heard their voice calling them from just beyond the tree line. And then, "It's wearing my face."

Alaska: The Haunting of Soapy Smith's Saloon

In 1897, Skagway wasn't a town—it was a festering wound on the edge of the continent. A rapidly swelling boomtown of desperate men and false promises, its mud-choked streets swallowed boots whole, the mire so deep that wooden walkways were thrown down in panic to keep people from sinking knee-deep. Buildings rose like rotted teeth—tall, narrow shacks with deceptive facades.

These fronts were meant to look proper while the backs sagged and bled into the mud. Tents and shanties filled every open space, their canvas walls thin as breath, doing little to keep out the wind or the stink of sweat, blood, and rot. Skagway was not built to last. It was built to *take*. To lure in the foolish and the hopeful and strip them bare.

The Klondike Gold Rush had opened a wound in the land, and the miners came pouring through it—thousands of them, chasing fortune into the teeth of the Yukon. But behind them came something else. Something colder.

His Name was Jefferson Randolph "Soapy" Smith

He came dressed in civility—a bowler hat, a smart coat, a voice like polished silver. But underneath was decay. He was a parasite born from a once-prosperous Southern family, turned into a predator by poverty and war. His past was lined with scams and corpses, none more famous than the "prize soap racket"—selling bars of soap with fake cash prizes, his own men posing as winners to bait the crowd. A thousand-dollar con wrapped in a dollar's worth of charm.

When he came to Skagway, it was like poison hitting an open wound.

Soapy opened his saloon and, with it, his empire. Fake telegraphs charged desperate miners to send messages that would never leave town. Rigged games bled them of their gold. His gang worked in shadows, whispering promises and threats. He bribed the weak, corrupted the greedy, and laughed at the rest.

The Town had a Breaking Point

But towns have a breaking point. By the summer of 1898, the people had seen enough. A vigilante committee formed in secret, shadows gathering to fight a greater one. They tried to meet quietly, but Soapy got wind of it. On the night of July 8, he marched to the Juneau Wharf with a rifle in his hands and the stink of arrogance on his breath.

There, he met Frank Reid, one of the men who refused to be bought.

No one knows who fired first. The only thing that mattered was the end:

Soapy lay dead, a bullet through his heart. Reid followed, dying days later from his wounds. The saloon fell silent. The town breathed again. Soapy was dumped in the woods, buried with a pistol on his chest, as if even death feared what he might do without one.

And Then Came the Ghost

But death did not quiet him. Skagway still carries the weight of its past today, and Soapy Smith's Parlor still stands—a museum now, but the walls remember. Glasses rattle on the bar with no hand to touch them.

Footsteps echo where the floorboards sag in the dust.

And sometimes, from the back room, a low chuckle slips out, dry and knowing—like a man watching a con unfold. Visitors speak of an impeccably dressed man in a bowler hat with straggly hair, a curled mustache, and a dead man's grin. He appears momentarily, then vanishes, leaving behind only the scent of tobacco and something colder—something metallic.

Locals say he's still here, watching, waiting, brooding over what was stolen from him. He doesn't haunt out of guilt.

He haunts because he was never done.

And in a town built on deceit and blood, maybe Skagway never left him either.

Arizona: Bloodiest Cabin in Arizona

He Came to Stake a Fortune

Frederick Brunckow was a man of education, logic, and ambition. Trained in mining engineering at the University of Westphalia, he left behind the old world in 1850 to carve a future from the rock and dust of the American West. After years with the Sonora Exploring and Mining Company, he believed he had found the perfect place to stake his fortune—a quiet bend near the San Pedro River in what would later become the shadows of Tombstone.

He thought it was isolated. Peaceful. Untouched.

He built his cabin by hand—a modest adobe structure, tin-roofed, with a fireplace that glowed orange against the endless night. It was meant to be a base of operations, a home, a storehouse for silver and supplies.

Home.

Instead, it Became a Tomb

The First Killings – July 23, 1860

On a hot, windless day in July, Brunckow was murdered, along with two of his associates. Their deaths were not clean. They were butchered.

James Williams, a miner, had gone to Fort Buchanan for supplies. When he returned, the cabin was eerily silent. The front door was open. Inside, the shelves were overturned, and supplies were scattered like entrails. His cousin lay sprawled in the storehouse, stiff and pale, throat cut wide.

He ran for help. When soldiers arrived, they began to dig up the dead. They found John Morse, the crew's chemist, butchered outside the camp, and Brunckow's body—broken, crumpled near a mine shaft, his skull caved in with a rock drill.

The earth drank what it could of the blood.

The rest dried on the stones.

Only one man survived: David Brontrager, another cook, who claimed the Mexican laborers had turned on the others during Williams' absence. But no one was ever caught. The desert swallowed their names.

The blood stayed behind.

Soldiers buried the bodies hastily, the graves shallow, marked only by piled rocks.

The whispers began soon after.

Something lingered at Brunckow's Cabin. Something angry. Something hungry.

It is like a wound that never heals, yearning for an infection to spread so it can rot and take hold of a body. It feeds then on the corpse. Over the next three decades, at least twenty-one people died violently on or near the site.

Throats slit. Skulls broken. Bodies burned.

In 1874, the first U.S. Marshal of Arizona Territory, Milton Duffield, came to evict a squatter named James Holmes from the cabin. Holmes shot him dead. Left him in the dust.

In 1897, a group of outlaws argued over stolen gold from a Wells Fargo stage near the cabin. Five of them died, their bodies crumpled beside the ruins, still clutching guns, eyes wide in death.

They all died where Brunckow had died.

They all died bad.

There's Something Bad Out There

The adobe walls are mostly gone now, just crumbled ghosts of stone, but something remains.

Something restless.

Visitors hear shouts in the wind, voices pleading, sobbing, screaming.

Some report shadowy figures flitting between mesquite trees. Some say they were called by name—by a voice that wasn't there. One man fled in the night.

Something touched his throat and whispered in a language he didn't understand.

Some nights, a low hammering is heard. As if someone is still mining in the dark. It is as if Frederick Brunckow still hasn't left the shaft where his life ended.

You can go. You can stand in the ruins. It's public land.

But be warned: *You might be sorry to choose this remote location.*

Because of those voices?

Those shadows?

They don't just haunt.

They wait.

The Bloodiest Cabin in Arizona has never stopped bleeding. It devours pain like a hungry child wolfs down candy—gleeful, unblinking, uncaring.

And when the wounds begin to dry and flake like old scabs, it whimpers in the dark, starving for another bite, another scream… another offering.

Arizona: Something Watches in Canyon Diablo

In the high desert east of Flagstaff lies a place the earth tried to bury. Canyon Diablo, they called it. Devil's Canyon. The name wasn't poetic. It was a grim warning.

In the late 1800s, when the Atlantic and Pacific Railroad reached the chasm and construction halted for a bridge, a settlement grew overnight. Not a town—a wound. A gash across the land filled with desperation, cruelty, and blood. Canyon Diablo never had a church.

It never had a school. But in its prime, it had fourteen saloons, ten gambling houses, and a cemetery with more graves than street addresses.

For four years, this place devoured men. It gulped them down whole and hacked out their bones. Shot in the street. Slashed in alleys. Hung from makeshift gallows as other men drank and laughed and placed bets on how long it would take them to choke.

Graves were dug in advance.

And yet—No One Stayed Buried.

When Canyon Diablo was thriving, strange things happened: Railroad workers went missing on their night shifts. No bodies were found—only boots and hats near the canyon rim, laid out like offerings to something no one dared name. Miners swore they saw eyes blinking from the cliff walls above the torchlight. Some said the eyes didn't reflect light at all—they swallowed it.

But what made this monster come long before the railroad?

The Navajo and Hopi people avoided the canyon for generations. They warned travelers away. They said it was a thin place where the boundary between this world and something far older was brittle—dry as bone, ready to crack.

They spoke of the Naaldlooshii, the Skinwalkers, and of faceless spirits that lived in the rocks—not ghosts, not men, but Watchers, Shadow Men, silent and waiting. Their eyes were black. Their forms unmoving. They were something older than man, crouched in the shadows of the cliffs—beings they called "The Watchers."

These spirits weren't ghosts of the dead but timeless entities—quiet, still, and cold as stone. They didn't speak. They didn't move. But if you wandered too close to the canyon edge at night, you might see one open its eyes, watching you from the rock itself.

Nobody Wanted to Listen

When the railroad men came, they laughed off the warnings. Then they started disappearing. One by one. Sometimes, a shovel was found. Or a lantern, still burning. Sometimes, nothing at all. Just a dull, unnatural silence and the creeping sense that someone was standing just behind you, too close, too still. The few who lived long enough to leave said the same thing: "It doesn't follow you. It waits. It knows you'll come back. Something is watching you."

After the bridge was finished and the railroad moved on, Canyon Diablo was left behind like an abandoned shanty house, where unspeakable things had happened and dried, crusty bloodstains still marked the walls. The saloons rotted. The brothels burned. The cemetery remains—stone markers for men who died too fast to remember their own names. Gunfights were so common that graves were dug in advance. Over thirty-five men were buried in the town's cemetery during its short boom—most unnamed, many shot, some hung by vigilantes. Men dueled at sunrise in the cemetery, standing on the fresh graves of soon-to-be replacements.

But even a ghost town casts a shadow. In the 1930s, a man named Peter Corman, an amateur geologist, hiked the area, searching carefully for meteorite fragments.

He was experienced, well-equipped, and methodical. He kept a journal. The last page read: "There is something in the canyon. It watches but doesn't blink. It doesn't breathe. But when the wind dies, I can hear it… thinking."

Peter was never found. His tent was zipped from the inside.

Heck yeah, go for a visit! It isn't damned! Or is it?

You can still go to Canyon Diablo. There are no signs, no services, and no rangers. It's all public land—but few choose to camp there.

Those who do report:

A presence—not a haunting, but a pressure, like the air thickens just before the sun goes down.

Footprints in the dirt at night. Human-shaped. Barefoot. Always approaching the fire. Never leaving it.

Silence that's too complete. Not just the absence of noise but the sense that something has silenced everything else.

No birds sing near Canyon Diablo after dusk. There's nothing commercial out there. No ghost tours. No tacky souvenirs. Just wind, sand, and that deep, silent chasm that once swallowed a town whole.

And those who've stood at the rim of the canyon on a windless night say the same thing:

"I think something is watching me."

Arkansas: Dead Bride of the River

In the fall of 1880, as the leaves withered and the skies turned gray, 21-year-old Gustavus Sanders, a quiet farmer from Pulaski County, married 16-year-old Martha, a girl known for her pale beauty and soft, distant voice. They wed atop the Natural Steps—a jagged staircase of ancient sandstone carved into the bluff above the Arkansas River.

It was a place of beauty… and foreboding.

The wedding was small, whispered about rather than celebrated. Some said Martha's family rushed the marriage. Others said Gustavus was already sick, the shadow of death tucked behind his hollow smile. Days after they exchanged vows, Gustavus fell ill.

Fever consumed him. By week's end, he was dead.

They buried him in the Natural Steps Shady Grove Cemetery, a patch of land veiled in cypress and gloom, tucked behind an old wooden church that creaked in the wind like a tired mourner. Martha was seen every day at his grave, unmoving for hours, lips parted as if whispering to the dirt.

The Girl Vanished

Then, one morning, she vanished. No screams. No notes. No footprints. Just emptiness in the cemetery.

Locals whispered that she had gone mad with grief—that she'd taken the same path they were married upon, down the slick, crumbling Natural Steps, and flung herself into the river's cold embrace.

Her body was never found.

But she never truly left.

To this day, residents of Natural Steps speak of the Bride in White. She returns on still October nights when the wind dies and the fog clings low.

She is seen drifting from the northeastern edge of the graveyard, dripping water as she goes, from the place where the church once stood, her gown luminous but muddy, sopping, and tattered, her face hidden beneath a veil soaked in shadow. She moves slowly—almost floating as if drawn by something no living soul can see.

Down the sandstone steps she goes, barefoot, silent, trailing the scent of river water and old roses. And mungy old rags. And just before she vanishes at the edge of the Arkansas River, some say she turns and looks.

Not to you, but *through* you.

And if you stand too long in the dark near those steps, you may hear the faint splash… and the sound of soft weeping echoing up from the river below.

Arkansas: A Ghost That Won't Die

A Light Flickers

There is a place in Arkansas where the swamp never sleeps. Deep in the pine woods outside the town of Gurdon, where twisted rails cut through black water and the mist clings like a corpse's skin long dead in the water, there is a light that burns for no one living. It flickers just beyond the bend, dancing above the train tracks, far from any road, too deep in the brush for headlights or lanterns.

It moves, searching as if lost.

And it began after something was taken. After something was left behind.

December 4th, 1931 – The Murder

It was during the leanest years of the Great Depression when Cora McClain appeared at the city marshal's door, drenched in fear and trembling. Her husband, Will McClain, a respected section foreman for the Missouri Pacific Railroad, had not come home. She kept glancing behind her as if expecting something to follow her out of the shadows.

The marshal acted quickly. McClain was not a man to vanish without cause. He was a creature of habit, always returning from his shift like clockwork. But this time, the clock had stopped. As investigators retraced McClain's steps, one man stood out—Louis McBride, a fellow rail worker. His answers were off.

His hands shook.

Beneath the weight of suspicion, he cracked.

The truth spilled out like blood on iron.

McBride had murdered McClain, striking him during an argument over job seniority. Anger twisted into madness. Desperation made him savage. He grabbed a shovel—then a railroad spike maul—and smashed McClain's skull again and again.

But McClain didn't die right away. He crawled, dragging his broken body into the woods. The ground told the story: a long trail of blood, fingerprints in the muck, scrapes where he clawed the earth, trying to get away.

His head had been crushed in multiple places.

His ribs were shattered.

But his hand never let go of his lantern. It was clutched in a death grip around the handle. And it would not let loose.

He died alone in the dark. And when they found him still clinging to that shattered lantern and took him to the morgue, not all of McClain went with the corpse.

Something stayed stuck to the tracks.

What Lingers

McBride was executed for the killing. The railroad moved on. But the swamp didn't forget.

Soon after the murder, the light appeared.

It floats above the tracks—sometimes white, sometimes blue. It weaves side to side, pulses like a heartbeat, and then vanishes before appearing farther down the rail again. Locals call it the Gurdon Light, and no one can explain it. Not swamp gas. Not headlights. Not tricks of the eye.

Because it moves like a man staggering through the brush.

Because it sways like a lantern clutched in a death grip in a dead man's hand.

Because it comes closer if you stare too long.

Beware, for the spirits of the murdered are restless and uneasy, and they are anything but mild-mannered after death. Their nature often transforms into a mix of rage, hostility, and a desire for revenge.

They may not always remember who harmed them.

But they seek to avenge themselves on anyone crossing their path.

Some say it's McClain, forever searching for a way home. Others believe something worse—that death twisted his soul, leaving behind not the man he was… but the rage, the fear, and the pain of dying alone in the mud. And that is what stuck to the tracks.

And such spirits?

They are not kind.

They do not remember who killed them.

They only remember the killing.

And they are eager to return the favor.

So, if you find yourself in the pine shadows beyond Gurdon and see the light hovering near the tracks, do not follow it.

It might spark your curiosity. It may seem harmless.

But it's not.

It's the light of the murdered.

And it is not done with us yet.

California: Wineville Chicken Farm Murders—Some Are Still There

In the 1920s, Wineville, California, was nothing more than farmland stretched thin across sunburned soil. Remote. Isolated. A place where screams could vanish in the wind. That isolation made it the perfect place for a terrible kind of evil to take root. Gordon Stewart Northcott, his mother Sarah Louise, and his young nephew Sanford Clark moved from Canada. They set up a modest chicken ranch on the outskirts of Wineville.

But behind the fences, something else was growing. Something grotesque.

Northcott was soft-spoken, even delicate in appearance. He was often seen gazing into mirrors, smoothing wisps of thick black hair with a wetted palm. He kept lip balm in his pocket and reapplied it compulsively as if preparing for a performance no one was meant to see. But behind the preening charm was a predator—calculated, cold, and cruel beyond reckoning.

He lured children to the ranch. And he killed them.

At least three boys were murdered. That much is certain. But investigators suspected the number could be far higher—possibly twenty or more. Their bodies were never all recovered. Many remain unaccounted for, their bones lost beneath the soil. On March 10, 1928, nine-year-old Walter Collins disappeared in Los Angeles after his mother, Christine, sent him to a movie.

In May of that same year, brothers Lewis (12) and Nelson Winslow (10) vanished while walking home from a model yacht club meeting in Pomona.

The Truth Unravels

The Los Angeles Police Department, already entangled in corruption scandals, mishandled the Collins case disastrously—returning the wrong child to his mother and then having her committed to a psychiatric hospital when she insisted he was not her son. The truth unraveled quickly. That summer, Sanford Clark confided in his sister Jessie. Northcott killed boys, he said. The ranch was not a ranch—it was something else. It was something horrid.

Authorities raided the property. There, buried beneath chicken coops and mounds of disturbed dirt, they found scattered human remains.

Bones. Bits of flesh.

Stray shoes.

It was enough to confirm the horror but not enough to give names to all who had died there.

Northcott was arrested, tried, and hanged at San Quentin in 1930.

But the land… never recovered.

Even now, strange things happen where the murders occurred. There are no historical markers, no plaques to speak the names of the dead. But locals know the place. And they avoid it. A metallic clanging is sometimes heard at night, like wire fencing struck by unseen hands.

Soft crying—childlike, low, sometimes in clusters—drifts through open fields where no one stands.

And then there's the smell—faint, sour, unmistakable.

Rot, where nothing is buried. A stench that clings.

People speak of the sensation of being watched. Not from above—not from windows or treetops. But from *below*. As though something on the ground… or beneath it… follows them step by step. Something low. Patient. Remembering.

And it's not just the dead. Some say Northcott himself never left. He walks again along old Wineville Road, his steps drawn back to the only place he ever had power. He walks the field at dusk, where the last light slips behind the hills.

They say his smile comes easily now. Pink-lipped.
Remembering.

The ranch is gone. Paved over in places. Portions are now equestrian paths; some stretches remain fenced but publicly visible.

But the horror hasn't faded.

The dogs won't go near.

The locals won't linger.

The sky over that stretch of land feels heavier than it should. Because no one knows how many children died there. No complete list was ever released.

Not all remains were recovered.

Not all souls were put to rest.

And the unspoken fear is this:

Some are still there.

Beneath the dirt. Still waiting to be found.

And Gordon Stewart Northcott is, too, slicking back his thick black hair with one wetted palm while applying lip balm to his pink lips with the other.

And as he smacks his lips together, he is thoughtfully, playfully watching you.

California: Preston Castle—The Blood in the Bricks

Preston School of Industry in the Sierra foothills of California opened in 1894. Framed as a reform school for juvenile boys ages 12 to 24, it stood like a promise of salvation—but delivered something far closer to damnation. At its peak, the school housed 800 boys and employed 200 staff. Behind its towering red walls, discipline was swift and brutal. Corporal punishment. Isolation. Humiliation. Some came to be reformed.

Others never left.

It rises like a fever dream above the dry hills, cast in blood-red brick, its peaked towers catching the sun like the edge of a blade. But when the sun sets, Preston Castle changes.

The light flees from its windows.

The wind coils through the halls.

And the basement begins to stir.

Locals do not linger after dark.

They don't need ghost stories.

They remember.

The Murder of Anna Corbin

In 1950, Anna Corbin, the 52-year-old head housekeeper, was found murdered in the castle basement. She was not just staff—she was beloved. A second mother to the boys. The one who treated them like children, not inmates.

It must have felt like a betrayal from the building itself. On the morning of her death, housekeeper Lillian McDowell and a young inmate named Robert Hall noticed a trail of blood leading from Anna's office to the decontamination pool room, where new inmates who came to Preston School of Industry were once forced to swim across to disinfect. When they forced open the locked door, they found Anna's body, brutally beaten, her skull fractured, her neck bruised and cinched with a length of hemp cord. She'd been wrapped in a rug like a discarded piece of trash. The violence wasn't impulsive.

It was ritualistic. Cold. Intentional.

A volatile boy named Eugene Monroe was arrested. He had blood on his shoes. Blood on his belt. A known history of violence. He had once attacked another staff member. But after three trials, he was acquitted. The case was never solved. And Monroe's name surfaced in other tragedies:

- In 1947, 17-year-old honor student Vesta Sapenter was found strangled in her bedroom.
- In 1951, Dorothy Waldrop, 22 and pregnant, was found dead—strangled, her body posed unnaturally.

But nothing stuck. Monroe walked free.

The boys and the staff knew. They always knew.

Something was wrong in that place.

And whatever it was—it didn't leave when the gates closed.

The Bricks Remember

When Preston was built, its bricks were not made locally. They were fired at San Quentin and Folsom, molded and handled by murderers, thieves, and violent men using sandstone quarried six miles from Ione.

Some say the curse began there—when bloodied hands pressed the clay, and rage and grief were baked into the walls. It's not superstition. It's history.

A building raised by the condemned, meant to cage the damned. Is it any wonder it breathes hate?

The Haunting That Followed

The school shut its doors in 1960. The building was left to rot. Nature came in through the windows.

But something else never left.

Footsteps echo on the top floor—when no one is there.

A woman in an old-fashioned uniform descends the staircase—only to vanish before the final step.

In the laundry room, where a boy was once crushed beneath a press, visitors report ice-cold air and the sensation of their limbs being weighed down.

And in the basement, where Anna died, the horror sharpens. People feel watched. They smell iron and mildew—the stench of blood that won't wash away.

Whispers drift through the air, not like voices, but like breath trying to form a word.

In 2004, a preservation volunteer fell down the basement stairs. He swore something grabbed his shoulder—not to steady him, but to pull. He wouldn't say what he saw. He quit the next day.

What Haunts Preston Castle

It's not just one ghost. It's not just Anna.

It's the weight of unspoken cruelty, of punishment mistaken for order, of children broken in silence.

It's the echo of Monroe's footsteps.

The boys who disappeared.

The ones who came out different—eyes empty, hands always trembling.

It may come from the very stone. The bricks were built by killers. Fired under heat. Hardened in hate. And now, they pulse with something living.

There's something in the basement.

It waits where the light cannot reach.

It remembers everything.

And it is not done.

You can visit today. Walk the halls. Descend the stairs.

But if you feel breath on your neck down there, if the air tightens and your skin prickles—*do not turn around. Run!*

Colorado: The Thing That Went Bump In the Night

In the autumn of 1941, Philip and Helen Peters lived on West Moncrieff Place, a quiet, tree-lined street nestled in one of Denver's most genteel neighborhoods. The houses were modest but well-kept, hedged in tidy lawns and trimmed hedgerows. It was the place where neighbors looked out for each other, windows glowed warmly in the early evening, and locked doors were more formality than necessity.

There's No Place Like Home

Philip, 73, was retired. A gentle man, he taught music with his wife and was a respected member of the Denver Guitar Club. Helen was recovering in the hospital from a fractured hip. During her absence, Philip kept up his routines—visiting his wife daily, eating with friends, and returning each night to the house they had shared for decades.

He never suspected that during those quiet hours, he was not alone. The home had another occupant—unseen, unheard, and watching.

On October 17, 1941, Philip Peters returned from the hospital earlier than usual. He stepped into the kitchen, expecting the silence of an empty house.

But the silence was broken.

Someone was there.

He came face-to-face with a man bent over his refrigerator.

The man turned. Then he attacked.

With a cast iron stove shaker pulled from the oven, the intruder bludgeoned Philip to death. Blow after blow fell with bone-cracking finality. The kitchen—once a quiet place for breakfast and music practice—was left spattered and still.

When concerned neighbors noticed the shades drawn and the house dark, they called the police. What they found was horrifying: Philip's body, crumpled and cold. But there was no forced entry. No signs of robbery. Nothing stolen, nothing broken.

A crime with no suspect and no exit.

The murderer had vanished.

Months later, Helen Peters returned home from the hospital—grieving, healing, and alone.

But the house was not empty.

She began to notice oddities.

Drawers slightly ajar. Furniture shifted.

Food went missing from the pantry.

Her clothing appeared disturbed, and her blankets moved—as if someone had made a bed and then vanished again.

It was easy to dismiss at first.

She was elderly. Recovering.

But then came the sounds.

Heavy footsteps. Muffled thumps.

Whispers in walls that held no voice. Neighbors heard them, too. A shape in the upstairs window. A face half-seen, gone too fast to follow. The police returned, skeptical but willing.

They searched. They waited.

And Then They Saw Him.

From a narrow ceiling panel above a closet, a hand emerged. Then, a pale, thin arm. Officers ripped the door open and hauled the man into the light.

His name was Theodore Edward Coneys. Coneys was 59 years old. A gaunt, brittle man with sunken eyes and long, trembling fingers. He had once met Philip Peters through the Denver Guitar Club. Years earlier, Coneys had visited the Peters's home as a guest.

On the night he returned, the house had been empty—and he had let himself in.

In a hallway closet, he found a trapdoor barely three feet high that led into an attic crawlspace just 36 inches tall. Filled with cobwebs, insulation, and dust, it was more coffin than room.

But Coneys claimed it as his own.

He lived there for months. Each night, while Philip slept, Coneys crept down from the ceiling, a wraith in threadbare socks, scavenging for food, drifting from room to room.

He heard everything.

Saw everything.

Learned their routines. He could have left.

But he didn't.

And when he was discovered, he killed.

After the murder, Coneys returned to the attic. The police had searched the house. More than once. But they never looked up. While Helen Peters mourned, while the neighbors whispered, while detectives puzzled over the impossible crime, Coneys lay just above them, listening.

Waiting.

He was still there when they finally dragged him out.

He hadn't left. He hadn't even planned to.

He confessed easily. Almost proudly.

He said he felt entitled to the house, to the warmth, the food, the silence. He said he never meant to kill, but he didn't sound sorry.

He was sentenced to life in prison.

The Press Called Him the Denver Spider-Man for the Cobwebs in the Little Crawlspace He Inhabited.

But to those who remember the case, he was something worse. He was a ghost that breathed.

A shadow that bled.

A man who became a myth—not because he vanished, but because he hid too well.

There are no paranormal claims tied to the house.

No glowing figures.

No haunted tours.

Just *things* that go bump in the night and the fact that for nine months, a killer lived above the ceiling. The victim never heard him coming.

They say it was an isolated case. A one-time horror.

But attics are still dark. Closets still narrow.

And floorboards still creak in the night.

So, check your locks. Listen closely.

Because it isn't just the dead that we should fear.

It's also the living ones who know how to hide.

I'll say it once more, did you remember to lock the door tonight?

Colorado: The Dead Rise in Ludlow

They Return to Remind Us

Some ghosts do not merely linger—they press back, dragging sorrow and accusation behind them. They do not flicker or fade.

They scratch. They wail.

They claw their way into the present not for comfort but for consequence.

And in Ludlow, Colorado, they have every reason to rise.

They Were Kicked Out of Their Homes

In the fall of 1913, a tent colony sprang up in the wind-ripped scrublands of southern Colorado, just 18 miles northwest of Trinidad. Over 1,200 striking coal miners and their families, evicted from company housing, gathered there under the banner of the United Mine Workers of America. They wanted fair wages. Safe working conditions. The right to organize without being crushed by the boot of the Colorado Fuel and Iron Company—John D. Rockefeller's company.

The miners dug in. They chose their location carefully, flanking critical rail lines and roadways to cut off strikebreakers.

But they placed more than picket lines in the path of the company.

They placed children. Wives. Entire families.

And the company responded. First, with private detectives. Then, with the Colorado National Guard.

Then, on April 20, 1914, with fire.

The Attack Began Before Dawn

Machine gun emplacements on the nearby ridge tore through the canvas shelters.

Men fled. Women screamed.

Children hid in root cellars dug beneath their tents.

The gunfire didn't stop for ten hours.

By dusk, the tents had been set ablaze.

And beneath one burned tent, in a single root cellar, they found thirteen bodies.

Two women. Eleven children. All burned.

All asphyxiated. Some were so small their bones fused to each other in death. Congress held hearings. The press raged. Rockefeller offered no apology. No National Guard officer was ever convicted.

No justice was delivered.

What was left was a scar on the land. A wound soaked in soot and silence. And silence, in places like Ludlow, has a way of curdling into something else.

The Ludlow Memorial Site Stands on Open Ground.

There are no fences. No locked gates. You may stand precisely where the massacre occurred. You may walk to the cellar—the death pit—where the children died. It is preserved. It is real. And it is not still.

People come for history. They leave with something else.

- Whispers drift beneath the wind, low and urgent, where no voices speak.
- Soot-covered women clutching bundled shapes are seen walking between the markers, only to vanish before they reach the road.
- On windless days, ash flutters, settling on cars, hands, and memorial plaques.
- The feeling of suffocation comes in waves—especially near the cellar. One visitor called it "the pressure of grief itself—like the land remembers what we try to forget."

In 2003, a group of amateur historians brought recording equipment. They expected wind, static, and birdsong. They recorded a woman's voice crying out, faint but persistent.

A linguist later suggested the language was Croatian or Greek—spoken by many miners who died that day.

At night, the stories turn stranger. Visitors have reported tiny handprints appearing on their car windows.

One woman left a stuffed bear for the lost children at the edge of the marker. When she returned an hour later, the toy had been moved to the cellar gate—soaked through, though the skies had been dry all day.

Some say a figure waits inside the cellar, visible only in photographs, where its outline can be seen curled among the stones.

Others have heard a slow rhythm echoing from the pit—like something breathing beneath the ground.

It is not a haunted house. There is no guide. No ticket.

Only a monument of stone. And the memory of fire.

What haunts Ludlow is not folklore.

It is grief, disfigured by time.

It is rage, made hollow and cold.

And it walks.

And it watches.

And it waits.

Connecticut: The Reef Takes at Penfield Lighthouse

Off the coast of Fairfield, Connecticut, in Long Island Sound, there stands a solitary lighthouse on a reef known as Penfield Reef Lighthouse. This lighthouse features a wooden-frame tower combined with a keeper's dwelling. It was built to protect passing vessels from the dangerous shallows of Penfield Reef. Over the centuries, this reef has caused the destruction of many ships, battering them against the hidden rocks beneath the dark waters.

And, as those who know the stories will tell you, *it holds on to what it takes. And when it returns it, it is usually dead.*

The Keeper Who Never Came Home

On December 22, 1916, Lighthouse Keeper Frederick A. Jordan, age 38, prepared to make a short crossing to the mainland. He had been relieved of duty by his assistant, Rudolph Iten, for the holidays and hoped to join his family for Christmas. Jordan packed a small satchel of handmade gifts and stepped into his dory. The water was cold. Winds were rising, but still, he rowed—pulling against the outgoing tide, hoping to beat the storm gathering in the west.

At 2:00 p.m., the sky snapped open. Gale-force winds tore through the Sound, and waves rose like iron hands. One struck hard—capsizing the boat. Rudolph Iten watched helplessly from the lighthouse windows as Jordan fought the water, then disappeared beneath it.

His empty boat washed ashore four days later.

Jordan's body was not found until the following March. He was buried quietly. But he did not rest.

The Figure on the Stairs

Iten, absolved of wrongdoing, remained at the lighthouse as the keeper. Winter passed. But something changed in the air around the tower.

One night, during a storm, Lighthouse Keeper Iten was stirred from his sleep by an odd sensation—as though someone was in the room with him. He rose from bed and saw it: "A gray, phosphorescent-covered figure emerged from the room formerly occupied by Fred Jordan," Keeper Iten would later recount to reporters.

"It hovered at the top of the stairs… and then disappeared into the darkness below."

Iten shouted to his assistant. The reply came from the lantern room: no one else was nearby.

Still uneasy, Iten descended the stairs and discovered the logbook had been moved—placed open on a table, the page turned to December 22, 1916. The day Jordon had drowned.

A Spirit That Will Not Leave

The sightings did not stop.

Over the years, other keepers saw the same figure—gray, silent, always watching from the shadows. The light in the tower sometimes faltered or flared without cause. Supplies were found moved. Lanterns lit themselves. Windows unlatched. Some claimed the temperature dropped instantly in Jordan's old room.

In 1942, two boys were pulled from the water after their boat overturned near the reef. They told their rescuers that a man had lifted them to safety—a man in an old-fashioned uniform, who vanished before they could thank him.

When shown photographs, they pointed to a portrait of Fred Jordan.

The Reef Remembers

There is an old sailor's saying passed between generations on the Sound: "What the reef takes, the reef will give back." But not always as it was. Some who pass the lighthouse at night swear they still see movement behind the glass—a man pacing alone, still keeping watch. A lone keeper who never reached the shore.

A man who rowed out into the wind and found something waiting below that he could not escape.

   He gave his life to the lighthouse.

   Now, the lighthouse keeps him.

Delaware: To Most it was just a Crooked Road...With a Ghost

It was just an Old Crooked Road—

The Old Baltimore Pike runs crooked through the Delaware woodlands, a centuries-old scar laid down before 1720. It once cut its way from Elkton to Christiana, a rough thread of earth and stone. By the time of the American Revolution, it had become a key passage for armies and kingsmen, patriots and traitors, horses, and death. It was walked by George Washington.

Rolled beneath the carriage wheels of Thomas Jefferson.

But few remember the man who died there, faceless and unclaimed.

And fewer still know that he never truly left.

The Crooked Road had an Ancient Bridge—

At the heart of this trail stood a simple wooden bridge stretched over the Christiana River—a patchwork of planks and logs built near the two-story stone house of Thomas Cooch, whose mill and farm gave the crossing its name—Cooch's Bridge.

To the modern eye, there is nothing exceptional about the place. A slope of road. A rustle of corn. A bridge weathered by time and storm. But on September 3, 1777, that ground drank in blood. And something below it shifted.

There was an Ambush at the Crooked Road with the Ancient Bridge—

British troops, bolstered by Hessian mercenaries, moved up the road from Elkton under cover of early light, bound for Philadelphia—the symbolic heart of the colonies. American riflemen were waiting for them in the thickets beyond the bridge, crouched in silence with muskets drawn.

The ambush was sudden. The woods erupted.

What followed was Delaware's only Revolutionary War battle—a brutal, all-day engagement remembered as the Battle of Cooch's Bridge. By dusk, the Americans were out of ammunition. The forest rang with the scrape of bayonets and blades. A fog of gunpowder and blood settled on the old toll road.

Just beyond the battlefield, near the Welsh Tract Baptist Church, the toll was taken. The church, a plain brick structure built in 1746 by Welsh settlers, stood firm amid chaos. But its east wall was struck. A British cannonball—fired from across the low fields—tore through the building's shuttered window and exited through a window on the west side.

But before the cannonball left the grounds, it found something else. No more than twenty yards away, a mounted American scout was caught mid-turn in the churchyard. The cannonball struck him in the neck—severing his head from his body in a single instant. His horse bolted. His head landed near the east wall.

Neither were recovered.

The Ambush at the Crooked Road with the Ancient Bridge Made a Ghost—

That should have been the end. But it wasn't.

For nearly 250 years, stories have passed from farmer to surveyor, from soldier to commuter, from one generation to the next: A rider in a Revolutionary War uniform, headless, crosses the battlefield path before vanishing beneath the trees—a figure galloping along Welsh Tract Road silhouetted against the highway in the fog. A blood-choked scream echoes from the cemetery on still nights. Travelers pull to the side of the road, waylaid by a sudden, freezing gust—only to find nothing and no wind. Witnesses describe the horseman not as theatrical but slow and searching. He does not chase. He simply moves forward, over and over, toward Cooch's Bridge… then vanishes.

In the 1980s, a construction crew working near the I-95 overpass claimed they saw "a man on horseback riding through the fog where there's no road." They reported it to the police. The officers found no tracks. But the oldest worker—quiet, superstitious—simply said: "He's still looking."

Some believe it was an American corporal named Charlie Miller, recorded as missing after the skirmish, presumed killed. Others say it was a British scout dressed in white to mimic a ghost, who was ironically shot through the head by frightened Americans.

No grave has ever been found.

No marker names him.

But he rides still, they say.

The battlefield is now a mix of protected land, asphalt, and exhaust—but spirits are not bound by development. The blood in the soil is still there. And the bridge—old as the bones beneath it—still trembles when fog drapes the fields.

So, if you walk that path at dusk, the woods are too silent, and the air turns still, listen.

You may hear the sound of hooves.

Not rushing.

But relentless.

Because the dead man never reached the other side.

Florida: Haunting End of Ed "Bloody" Watson

There are places in Florida where the air is thick enough to drown in. The Everglades hold more than water and rot. They hold secrets—long buried, half-sunken, never entirely still. And in the twisted mangroves of the Ten Thousand Islands, something evil once took root in human skin. His name was Edgar J. Watson, born November 11, 1855, in South Carolina to a drunken father whose fists served as instruction.

His life began with cruelty—and he carried it forward like a legacy, sharpening it across decades, across states, across bodies. He became known by a name whispered like a curse: *Bloody Watson.*

He came to Florida not to change but to vanish—to hide inside the swamp's lawless corridors and build something from blood. What he built instead was terror.

The Devil Takes a Seat

Watson was not just a killer. Many men were killed. But there was something else in him—a rot in the soul, old and smiling. People said it felt like the devil had discovered a place to play and a mate to dance with, and that playground and bride was Ed Watson. "The devil himself rode into the Glades on Watson's back," one old settler once said. "And then he got off and made himself at home."

Watson planted sugarcane near Chokoloskee and made his fortune. But crops weren't all that sprouted from the wet soil. The dead appeared there, too.

People went missing. Workers. Women. Families.

Those who crossed him didn't come back. Those who demanded pay weren't seen again. And the Everglades, patient and bottomless, took them all.

His Victims Were Many. Few Were Named.

Belle Starr, the infamous Bandit Queen, was reportedly shot by Watson in Oklahoma after refusing to dance with him. Some say it was personal. Some say she knew too much. Officially, her murder is unsolved.

Adolphus Santini, throat slit. Watson paid him $900 to stay quiet.

Hannah Smith, a large woman Watson murdered near Chatham Bend. A child witnessed him burying her 300-pound body. The shallow grave failed to hide her—the flesh of her leg stuck out from the dirt like the swamp itself had rejected her burial.

Quinn Bass was murdered over a land dispute. Watson claimed self-defense. No one dared dispute him.

Leslie Cox, a drifter or a friend—or a scapegoat. Watson blamed him for other murders. Cox vanished. No one ever proved who did it.

And so many laborers they cannot be counted— black men, poor men, nameless men—who showed up with callused hands and left in silence when they came to collect their pay. Some say he paid them in bullets. Some say their bodies still float beneath the lily pads.

The Tucker Family Changed Everything

What broke the silence was a family.

The Tuckers were farmers known and liked in the Chokoloskee settlement. But they sat on land Watson wanted. When they refused to leave before their harvest came in, he murdered them—all of them, some say children included—and dumped their bodies in the river like trash. But murder has a limit. Even the Everglades cannot hold in the stench forever.

Judgment at the General Store

The people of Chokoloskee had enough. And it seemed the devil inside old Watson was also ready to leave his human form. It must have rounded up all the ghosts the man had murdered along the way to watch the killer get his due. Because the tide changed that day for the town.

On October 24, 1910, the locals met him at the Ted Smallwood Store, where he had come to trade and bully. They were waiting. Watson reached for his shotgun. Oddly, the weapon misfired. The mob's guns did not. They opened fire. They shot him again and again until the man fell still. And then they kept shooting. So many bullets tore through him that his autopsy reportedly yielded a coffee can's worth of lead. It was over. Ed Watson was dead. But the thing inside him? That didn't die. It clung to his ghost instead. Waiting for its next prey, its mate.

A Presence That Won't Go Away

The Ted Smallwood Store still stands. Preserved, quiet. But never still. Visitors report cold drafts that come without wind and the constant sensation of being watched by something not fully human. The scent of gunpowder is sharp and sudden. And sometimes—only sometimes—a man is seen just outside the door, his boots wet, his face unreadable, watching.

Some say it's Watson. Others say it's the thing that used to live in him, still pacing, still hungry. They buried the man. But they never buried the hate. And the devil? The devil remembers— Remembers how good it felt to dwell in a soul that never fought back, a soul foul, rank with rot, and ripe for ruin. That was home.

A comfortable place where darkness didn't need to hide. And now, he waits.

He—and everything that hunts with him— are searching for souls just like Watson's.

So, step inside the store. Let the floorboards groan.

Let the air test your breath. And ask yourself: Is your heart pure? Or have you done something, even tiny, bad?

Because if it's not...pure... prepare for a long, gruesome ride. The devil climbed out of dead Watson, and he is looking for a new bride.

Florida: The Haunting of St. Augustine Lighthouse

It rises out of the mist like something too old to fall—the St. Augustine Lighthouse, black-and-white spiral ribs twisting toward the sky like bone. For over 150 years, it has stood at the edge of Anastasia Island, where sea winds hiss through the trees, and the land never forgets the dead.

It is beautiful. It is historic. And it is very, very haunted.

There is a sound in the lighthouse soft, just beyond hearing. It is not the ocean. It is not the wind. It is the past, grinding like rust beneath the floorboards, whispering through the stairwell. It has a voice, though it does not speak. It giggles.

The Cart Ride to Nowhere

In 1873, Superintendent Hezekiah Pittee brought his family to live on-site during the construction of the new lighthouse tower. Four children: Mary Adelaide, Eliza, Edward, and little Carrie. The island was wild and unpolished then—sand, sawgrass, half-built brick, and a supply cart that ran from the coast to the construction yard.

The cart became a plaything. A rollercoaster on rails.

They rode it laughing, again and again, to the edge of the sea.

And then one day—July 10, 1873—the wooden stop block was missing. The cart did not stop.

It plunged off the end of the tracks and into the water. The girls—Mary Adelaide (15), Eliza (13), Carrie (4), and a 10-year-old laborer's daughter—were trapped beneath.

The tide rose.

The laughter stopped.

Only Carrie survived.

The rest never walked the beach again.

The Giggles That Never Ended

Time passed. The lighthouse was completed in 1874. But the children never truly left. Today, tourists hear giggles echoing down the high tower's stairwell.

Tiny footsteps race across the floor above them—only to discover the level is empty.

Staff lock the doors at night and return to find them wide open.

Some say the smell of salt water and old iron creeps in through the walls, even on dry days.

"You chase those laughs thinking it's a group of kids," one guide said. "And then you realize—you're the only person on the stairs."

One keeper, James Pippin, quit without notice. He told his supervisor: "I won't spend another night in that place. Not with them still moving around upstairs."

More Than Children Died Here

The lighthouse is older than its 19th-century foundations. It sits on the bones of Spanish and British watchtowers. Men died defending them. Sailors drowned in the shallows below.

A keeper named Joseph Andreu fell from the tower while painting—his body snapped by the stone base, his blood soaked into the brick.

Sometimes, Andreu's shadow is seen watching from the top of the tower, gazing out across the sea.

A woman once paused on the metal staircase. Her shoelace caught the step. She stumbled. When she looked down—her laces were tied in a perfect knot.

Another visitor took a photo at the base of the spiral. Later, zooming in, he saw a woman's face in the shadows behind him.

There had been no one else on the stairs.

The Basement That Won't Burn

During the 1970s, a fire destroyed part of the keeper's house. The basement remained untouched. Today, it is the coldest place on the property. Workers speak of a black shape moving from wall to wall. Guests descend the stairs and report a feeling of being watched so intensely they must leave.

"I heard a whisper behind me," one woman uttered. "Not words. Just breath. And then something brushed my neck."

One staff member said it best: "There are places in that house where you're not alone, even if you're the only one there."

Not Every Light Guides You Home

The St. Augustine Lighthouse was built to save lives. But something else moved in with the bricks and salt and sorrow.

Something that doesn't want to be forgotten.

The laughter still echoes.

The steps still creak.

The light still shines.

But sometimes, when you're standing halfway up that endless spiral staircase, and the sea wind dies, and there's no one above or below—you'll hear the sound of a cart.

Rusty wheels. *Squeak-squeak.* Picking up speed. *Squeak-squeak.* Coming straight toward you. *Squeak-squeak. Squeak-squeak—*

And there's no board to stop it.

Georgia: The Dead Still Defend Fort McAllister

Thirty minutes south of Savannah, where the Spanish moss hangs too still in the heat, and the marsh never goes quiet, stands Fort McAllister—a fortress of sod and blood built on a plantation and soaked in misery. Rising above the slow, black flow of the Ogeechee River, the fort was constructed in 1861 to withstand naval assault. Earthworks thick with cannon. Salt-soaked winds. Trenches like open mouths. But no wall keeps out death.

The Murder of Major Gallie

On February 1, 1863, under relentless fire from Union gunboats, Major John B. Gallie moved like a ghost through the smoke, rallying his men across the dirt walls. He refused to seek cover. He would not be seen flinching. Even after a shard of shrapnel tore through his face, Gallie waved off medical attention.

"I'm still whole," he insisted, blood pouring down his jaw. "Let them come."

Moments later, another round struck him. It tore through his skull. Witnesses said he remained upright a moment too long—as if his body hadn't yet accepted it was dead—before collapsing beside the iron 32-pounder he had just fired. His head was mangled. He was no longer recognizable. He died in the dirt. That patch of earth never stayed the same.

Hell Behind the Walls

Fort McAllister repelled seven assaults during the war. It did not always win. In December of 1864, Union General William Tecumseh Sherman unleashed the final blow during his infamous March to the Sea. The battle lasted fifteen minutes—a red, brief scream of gunfire and cannon. Dozens of Confederate defenders were slaughtered in the trenches. Those who survived were thrown into cells. The fort became a makeshift prison, a crucible of fever, starvation, and hopelessness. The war ended, but the pain did not.

The Dead That Won't Leave

The Headless Major: They say Major Gallie is still there and never left the post he died while defending.

Visitors have seen him at night—a headless man in Confederate gray, pacing along the southern wall or standing silently near the rusted artillery where he fell. Some feel a sudden temperature drop, which doesn't belong in the Georgia heat. Others swear they hear footsteps, slow and steady, with nobody to cast the sound. Rangers don't talk about it unless you ask. *But they know.*

The Maimed Soldiers: On dark, fog-laced evenings, wounded men are seen dragging themselves through the brush—one missing an arm, another crawling with legs that bend the wrong way. Their faces are slack. Their mouths sometimes move. But no sound comes out.

The Phantom Cat: In the chaos of war, even animals weren't spared. "Tom Cat," the fort's beloved black feline mascot, was struck and killed by cannon fire during the Union attack. Now, long after the war, tourists report a black cat streaking across the parade ground—only for it to vanish mid-stride. Some claim they've felt it brush against their ankles, purring, though nothing is there when they look down.

When the Workers Fled

In the 1930s, Henry Ford funded the restoration of the historic site. But not all his workers stayed. Men hired to labor on the property refused to remain after dark. They complained of screams with no source, tools that moved on their own, and voices whispering through the walls, calling names none of them recognized.

"It ain't right here," one said, walking off the job. "They don't want it fixed."

Still on Guard

Fort McAllister may be a park now, a place for tours and trails. But it is still a fortress, not of wood or earth—but of memory, of blood, and of pain. The wind that blows across the Ogeechee sometimes carries more than salt. It carries a warning.

Come after sunset, and you may see them:

The watchman with no head.

The soldiers who never stopped crawling.

The cat who never stopped guarding.

They are still there. Still defending. Still trapped. *And they don't want you here.*

Georgia: Breakfast in Hell—The Haunting of Old Number 7

In the summer of 1900, McDonough, Georgia, was a postcard of Southern charm: tidy porches, church bells, and the iron heartbeat of the Southern Railway, which stitched Macon to Atlanta like thread across the land. It was a town built on rhythm—of trains, of harvests, of prayer. But something broke that rhythm on June 23rd, and McDonough never quite recovered.

It began with rain. And it ended with screams.

The Rain That Would Not End

For weeks, storms had soaked Henry County. The sky poured without mercy. Creeks became rivers, and rivers swallowed roads. The brick supports beneath the Camp Creek trestle began to erode, rotting beneath the tracks like a disease no one could see. But orders were orders.

Despite weather reports and warnings about the weakened rail line, the Old Number 7—a train bound north—was told to proceed. Engineer J.T. Sullivan was at the controls, filling in for a sick colleague. His voice was calm. His tone was dry. When a nervous passenger asked about the storm, he gave a half-smile and said: "We'll either be having breakfast in Atlanta... or Hell."

The Fall

At 9:45 PM, Old Number 7 pulled out of McDonough, chugging north through the dark woods. Ahead, the Camp Creek trestle was gone. Washed away. Erased. Only two rails remained, stretching over a 60-foot drop like skeletal fingers. Sullivan never had a chance.

As the train reached the bridge, the earth gave way. The locomotive plunged into the swollen blackness below, smashing into the water and twisted timber. The cars behind followed, crashing down like coffin nails. Witnesses miles away said they heard the screech of metal, followed by silence.

The Toll

Forty-eight souls were aboard. Nine survived.

Some drowned, trapped in the wreckage as the creek rose around them. Others burned—the passenger car caught fire after impact, flames hissing in the rain.

Bodies were pulled from the creek for days. Some were never found at all.

And J.T. Sullivan? They found him still clutching the brake lever, his face frozen—not in fear, but in resignation. He tried. But fate had already arrived.

The Ghosts Along the Tracks

The dead did not stay quiet.

Locals began hearing things near the site of the disaster—voices carried on fog, calling out station names or screaming for help.

A lantern light, seen bobbing along the old right-of-way, vanishes if approached. Some say they've heard the hiss of steam and the rattle of an old train passing in the dead of night.

But most disturbing are the apparitions. A soaked conductor, missing one hand, was seen limping toward McDonough station before vanishing into the trees.

A woman in a burnt dress, her mouth locked open as if still mid-scream.

Even in McDonough Town Square, where the corpses of those without identifying papers were laid out for families to identify them, ghosts have also been viewed.

And near the creek itself, a figure in an engineer's uniform has been witnessed staring into the water. Many believe it is Sullivan, cursed to replay the moment forever. Some say he wanders, still trying to stop a train that's long since fallen.

Others believe he was claimed by something darker.

After all…he named his destination.

A Place That Remembers

The death trestle is long gone, but the land remembers.

The air near Camp Creek grows still, unnaturally still. It's as if something is listening. And those who walk the trail after dark say they feel a pressure—like something riding behind them, just out of view. Perhaps it's the weight of the souls lost.

Or perhaps it's the train itself—still falling.

Over and over.

Forever.

So, if you ever visit McDonough and the storm clouds roll in heavy and low, take care where you walk.

Because Old Number 7 is still on the rails, somewhere in the dark. And breakfast in Hell might still be waiting.

Hawaii: Kasha at the Kaimuki House

In the sun-bleached neighborhood of Kaimuki, a residential area in Honolulu tucked among the gentle sway of palm trees and the whisper of trade winds, there once stood a house that held something ancient, something unnatural.

From the outside, the Kaimuki House was ordinary—just another clapboard frame sagging in the tropical heat.

But within its walls, something watched.

And when it chose to act, it did so with a hunger that made the soul recoil. Because that house, they say, was home to a Kasha.

The Fire Cart Spirit

In Japanese folklore, a Kasha is no mere ghost. It is a carrion demon—a spirit that appears as a stray black cat, slinking through alleys and gardens, biding its time. When death comes, it drags corpses to the underworld, sometimes animating them as puppets, other times feasting on them mid-transit. The name means "burning chariot," a grim image of its role as psychopomp, a conductor of souls to the afterworld, and a predator.

They say the Kaimuki House was built over the site where a Japanese immigrant murdered his entire family before taking his own life. Some say the earth beneath the house was already cursed. Others say the blood soaked into the foundation gave the Kasha a place to cling.

But either way, it waited. And then, it struck.

August 13, 1942 – When It Revealed Itself

Police were called to the Kaimuki home shortly after nightfall. A mother, frantic and screaming, claimed her children were being attacked by something she could not see.

Officers Moseley Cummins and Robert Ansteth found three siblings—a 10-year-old boy and his sisters, ages 18 and 20—huddled on a couch, howling in terror. The air inside the house was stifling. Heavy. And something else lingered—the acrid smell of sulfur, an odor long associated with spiritual corruption.

The mother tried to ward it off with ti leaves and Hawaiian salt, traditional protections against malevolent spirits. But it was no use.

"It's on the boy," she shouted. "It smelled him first."

Then the attack came.

The children were thrown against the walls by invisible hands. One girl collapsed to the floor, clutching her throat. The boy shrieked and clawed at the air. The police could do nothing. For over ninety minutes, the entity tormented the family—and the officers could only watch.

When they finally fled the house at 3 a.m., the mother turned to the officers and whispered: "Look... you have goose-pimples too."

They did.

1972 – It Came Back

Thirty years later, three teenage girls encountered something in the same area. While driving down Waialae Avenue, they were overcome with panic. One girl began choking, her hands clawing at her throat as if an unseen rope had been looped tightly around her neck.

A police officer arrived and attempted to pull her from the car—only to feel a cold, invisible hand grip his arm. He froze. The moment passed. But it wasn't over.

When the girl was moved to a patrol car, the engine refused to turn over. Nothing would start—until she was returned to her original seat. Moments after the girls resumed their drive, one was ripped from the vehicle and thrown onto the roadside. There were no hands. No attacker. Just force.

The House May Be Gone, But Something Remains

The original Kaimuki House was demolished in 2016. A clean, modern duplex stands in its place—white walls, manicured lawn, perfectly silent.

But locals know better.

They say the land itself remembers.

Some spirits are bound not to wood and nails but to suffering.

And that once a Kasha finds a place to feed, it never truly leaves.

People still walk wide circles around that corner of 8th Avenue and Harding, especially at night. Stray cats vanish from the area. And sometimes, just sometimes, people say they hear a voice in the dark—

Low, guttural, like something dragging a corpse across the tile.

Something old.

Something patient.

Something hungry.

Hawaii: Dead Curve—Where Urban Legend and True Horror Meet

Deep in the jungle-thick heart of Nuuanu Valley, where the mist clings low to the road and the rain never entirely stops, there is a bend they don't speak of lightly. A hairpin curve carved into the landscape like a scar. It was once a quiet road. It is quiet still. But now, the silence is different. They call it Morgan's Corner. At first glance, it's just a sharp turn along the old Nuʻuanu Pali Road under a canopy of green so thick it chokes out the sun.

But for decades, this patch of earth has been whispered about in gasps, not stories. A place where fact and legend merged like shadow and fog and where something unholy seems to have lingered after a real and brutal crime.

An Urban Legend Rooted in Real Death

An old story emerged, blurring with the facts: a couple's car stalled beneath a tree. The boy leaves for help. The girl stays behind. Later, she hears something scratching above the roof. It goes on and on until she finally steps outside and looks up—Her boyfriend hangs from the tree above her. His toes drag across the metal roof gently, endlessly—*Tip-tip. Tip-tip. Tip. Tip.*

The tale is made up—there is no record of this death. But it stuck because Morgan's Corner is the kind of place where lies grow in the same soil as truth, and the two become impossible to pull apart. Because death did walk here.

The Truth Buried in the Dirt

The curve is named after Dr. James Morgan, who once owned the home above the bend. But that is not what people remember. They remember the murder.

On March 11, 1948, two escaped prisoners—James Majors and John Palakiko—staggered through the soaked valley after fleeing from Oʻahu Prison. Hungry and desperate, they came upon the isolated home of Therese Wilder, a 68-year-old widow. She lived alone.

They broke in. They bound her. They stuffed a gag so deep in her throat that she suffocated slowly, writhing in her bed. They left her there like a discarded object. Dead.

Her body was not found until five days later—by then, the flies knew before the neighbors did.

The Haunting Echoes After

The crime ripped through Honolulu like a knife. Majors and Palakiko were quickly captured and sentenced to death, though their punishments were later reduced. But by then, the damage had already taken hold—not just in the legal record, but in the soil itself.

Because Morgan's Corner changed after that. Locals started to avoid the bend. Even in daylight, they said, something felt wrong. Too cold, too silent, too watched.

And Then the Stories Began

Drivers reported a woman in white standing just ahead in the road. She does not move. She does not speak. When headlights reach her, she is gone.

Couples parked nearby speak of sudden scratching sounds—faint at first, then louder, more insistent. Always above the car. Always something brushing the roof.

And in the deepest part of the night, some say you can hear the sound of rope stretching just behind the trees. Follow the noise, and you'll find nothing… but you'll feel something watching.

The Place Itself Remembers

Even after the roads were widened and the Morgan home demolished, the curve still feels cursed. A Honolulu police officer once told a reporter, off the record: "I won't stop there at night. I've seen her. Just once. And that was enough."

Others—paranormal researchers, hikers, even postmen—have felt it: a pressure on the chest, a sudden inability to breathe, the feeling that someone is behind you, just out of reach. And then there is the loud scream sweeping out of nowhere.

Some say the land swallowed the scream, and now it echoes on a loop.

So, if you ever find yourself driving through Nuuanu Valley, the mist creeps in low, and the rain softens your tires to silence… and you reach that bend—

Keep your windows up.

Don't stop.

And whatever you do—don't look in the rearview mirror.

Because Morgan's Corner doesn't forget.

And some dead things still walk at night. They are never truly buried in the dirt.

Idaho: Crybaby River

There is a stretch along the Snake River where the wind doesn't sound like wind—it sounds like weeping, mewling, sobbing. And if you stand still enough to hear it clearly, it becomes something worse. It becomes a child *crying*. That place is Massacre Rocks State Park, a corridor of jagged boulders and twisted basalt lining the riverbank like broken teeth. In the days of westward expansion, pioneers called this place by other names— "The Gate of Death." Some whispered it as "Devil's Gate."

And those who passed through with wagons and prayers often crossed themselves afterward, grateful only for surviving the crossing. But many did not survive. And some who died here never left at all.

Where the Rocks Remember Blood

The name Massacre Rocks is no accident. In August of 1862, along this jagged corridor, a clash between Shoshone warriors and Oregon Trail emigrants left dozens dead, their blood leeching into the sand while the river rolled on, indifferent. Some died by ambush. Others by panic. Some were buried in shallow graves.

But it was not just soldiers and settlers who perished here. Children died, too. Some from illness. Some from accident. And some—if the old stories are to be believed—were drowned deliberately by desperate mothers too broken by hunger, loss, and fear to carry them farther. *It is their cries that linger.*

The Water Babies

Along the Snake River, local lore tells of spectral infants, known as Water Babies, who haunt the shoreline like mist. These are *not* sweet ghosts. They are not gentle. They are something else entirely:

Infants drowned. Small mouths gasping. Tiny hands reaching. Souls that never found peace.

The legend says they rise and dance at twilight, their tiny pale forms flitting like candlelight along the riverbank. And always, always, the sound comes first: soft sobbing, a lullaby with no singer.

Some say the cries are a warning.

Others say they are a lure.

The Lure of the Crying Dead

Hikers and park rangers have whispered about strange sounds near the water—children's voices where no children were. Footsteps on dry stone. Splashing without source. More than one traveler followed the sound, thinking it was a lost child crying for help.

And some… don't come back.

They are found later, bloated and cold, pulled from the shallows by rescue teams. Their expressions are frozen in something that looks like wonder. Or horror.

"They always go in alone," one ranger said. "No footprints but their own. But sometimes… you can see tiny barefoot prints beside them. Just impressions in the mud. It's too small to be an adult. Too perfect."

Don't Follow the Sound

Today, Massacre Rocks is a state park. Families picnic there. Children play. But some places do not forget. Some rivers never give back what they've taken.

At twilight, the rocks turn black. The air grows heavy.

And the cries return. If you hear them—don't go looking. Because they want you to.

And if you answer them, if you step one foot into the water, you may feel a hand take yours.

Small. Cold. Delighted.

And then you'll dance too.

Just another whisper lost beneath the current.

Idaho: Lady Bluebeard—Black Widow Who Wouldn't Stay Dead

In Twin Falls, Idaho, where the wind pulls over the Snake River Plain in long sighs and the basalt shadows stretch unnaturally at dusk, there's a grave you might miss if you weren't looking for it. It's small. Unassuming. The name etched there is Anna E. Shaw. But beneath that stone lies Lyda Southard—church girl, serial killer, and perhaps the most dangerous woman ever buried in Idaho soil. *And some say she isn't buried deep enough.*

She married them and buried them.

She was born Anna Elizabeth Trueblood in Missouri in 1894. Her family raised her in prayer and respectability, but somewhere along the line, the shape of something darker took root. She changed her name to Lyda.

Changed it again when it suited her.

And over the next decade, she left behind a trail of coffins that grew cold before the ink on their insurance policies could dry.

She married Robert Dooley in 1912. He died three years later of so-called typhoid fever. Then his brother Edward—also dead. Then, William McHaffie, whose death was chalked up to influenza. Then Harlan Lewis was gone one month after their wedding. And finally, Edward Meyer, who died not even a season after saying "I do."

Each time, Lyda grieved politely. Each time, the insurance payouts landed directly in her pocket.

And each time, the doctors signed death certificates that didn't quite smell right. But it wasn't until Meyer's death that the mask cracked. Because Lyda didn't claim his policy—not right away. And grief? She wore it like a hat that was two sizes too large.

The Worms Beneath the Coffin Lid

When investigators returned to her old home, they found flypaper—the kind used in those days to trap pests. But soaked in water, the arsenic could be extracted. And arsenic was precisely what they found in the bodies of Lyda's former husbands, exhumed one by one, the flesh leached and pale with poison.

She was arrested. She was convicted of one death, though she left behind far more. She served her time in prison until she seduced another inmate into helping her escape. When caught again, she smiled for the camera.

She served the rest of her time and died quietly in Salt Lake City in 1958 at 65. But the dead don't always stay where they're planted.

The Grave That Sings

They buried her under her final alias—Anna E. Shaw—at Sunset Memorial Park in Twin Falls. A name forgotten. A life erased. A lonely, lonely grave.

But not long after her burial, people began to see a pale woman in old-fashioned clothes standing alone by her grave. She never speaks. She doesn't move when addressed. And then, she vanishes.

One groundskeeper, working late in the season, heard laughter behind him—low, musical, and wrong. He turned. No one. But the wind picked up, and he could swear it whispered:

"Till death do us part…"

She's Still Looking

Lyda was dead. But not so dead.

Some say her soul never settled because she was never punished for all she took. Some believe the devil was too scared to take her, so she lingers. But others suggest something more terrifying: That Lyda—clever, patient, and smiling—is still waiting.

And if she ever finds the right man again… she might just dig herself out.

Illinois: Bloody Gulch Murder

The land south of Dixon is quiet now, the gulch long overgrown, the stream just a whisper of water sliding through the roots. But the ground remembers. And sometimes, when the wind kicks up and the sky sours with rain, the soil gives up its secrets.

On September 18, 1885, Farmer James Penrose was driving cattle along that forgotten stretch of countryside when he caught sight of something pale in the creek bed. At first, it looked like a root or a bone.

It was a hand.

The fingers were curled, stiff, slick with rot, and reaching—not buried, but clawing upward. The shallow grave that had once hidden the body had been slowly undone by rain. The earth had tried to swallow what it could, but the corpse resisted.

The Boy in the Gulch

The body belonged to Fred Theil, age seventeen, a Bible book agent from Elgin who had vanished days earlier while working for Gately & Co. of Chicago. His job had been to walk the rural roads alone, offering faith door to door.

What they found in that gulch was no boy—it was a wreck.

The head caved in with blunt force.

The throat slashed from ear to ear.

His left hand was mangled, fingernails ripped from the bone.

Pockets turned inside out.

His gold watch and chain—gone.

His body, already crawling with teeny white maggots, had been shoved beneath the surface like rubbish. But the earth would partially spit it back out.

The Spade, the Chain, and the Man Who Lied

A farmer had seen a man walking that road alone—a man carrying a spade. That man was Joseph Mosse, a French-Canadian farmhand with no good alibi. When officers came for him, he smiled. But they watched as he palmed a gold chain and tried to fling it into the weeds.

He dropped a cigar holder, too—both belonging to the dead boy.

When they searched his trunk, they found a pair of blood-soaked trousers. A young woman came forward. She had walked half a mile with him. "He had the spade," she said, her voice flat. "He told me he didn't. But I saw it."

Back at the gulch, police recovered a blood-smeared stone and a knife. Mosse had hired a team that night and returned to his quarters long after midnight. By then, the gulch was quiet. The stream was still.

The killer was arrested, convicted, and sentenced to life in prison.

But Justice Doesn't Always Silence the Dead

If you think ghosts rise only when justice is denied—think again. Because in the decades that followed, strange stories began to bloom like mildew on the creek stones. Locals swore they saw a pale hand, caked in mud and worms, reach from the soil along the gulch during thunderstorms. Sometimes it beckoned. Sometimes it clawed. And once, in the black of a rain-heavy night, a traveler reported seeing a figure standing at the edge of the stream, its throat a yawning red grin.

And then, just as lightning split the sky—One local described the scene, "It vanished," he said. "But the water still rippled like something had crawled in."

There's no marker at Bloody Gulch. No signpost. But the ground knows where the blood is. And the hand still reaches, not for help—

but for someone to take down with it.

Illinois: Old Book and the Crying Tree—Peoria State Hospital

The dead do not always rest.

There is a place in Illinois where the ground is soaked not only with sorrow but with a silence that weeps. The Peoria State Hospital in Bartonville was once hailed as the model of compassion, where its superintendent, Dr. George Zeller, sought to treat the mentally ill with dignity at the turn of the 20th century. But no act of mercy can stop a good haunting.

The Grave Digger

He arrived in 1902—a mute man of unknown origin, unable to write, speak, or explain his past. The staff named him Manuel A. Bookbinder after the profession scribbled into a forgotten intake ledger. But soon, they simply called him Old Book.

He worked among the dead. As part of the asylum's burial crew, Old Book dug the graves, lowered the caskets, and wept for those the world had forgotten. He always leaned on one ancient elm tree, his shoulders trembling as he mourned—not with sound, but with motion as if the grief inside him could not be spoken, only lived.

That tree, where he stood, came to be known as The Crying Tree.

The Funeral That Shouldn't Have Happened

In 1910, Old Book died. And on the day of his funeral, the asylum gathered to pay respects to the quiet man who had wept for so many. As the casket was lowered into the earth, the pallbearers faltered—the coffin had grown unnaturally light. And then a sound came from the elm. "He was there," one nurse whispered afterward. "Leaning against the Crying Tree. Weeping."

Hundreds saw it—the apparition of Old Book, shaking with grief, watching his own funeral from a few feet away. The crowd gasped. A woman fainted. The minister dropped his prayer book. Dr. Zeller, the superintendent, ordered the casket opened. The lid was lifted slowly. And there he was—Old Book's corpse, still and cold, unmoved in death. But outside, the figure still wept.

The Tree That Wouldn't Die

After Old Book was buried, the Crying Tree began to rot. The grass around it withered. Birds no longer landed in its branches. And at night, staff reported seeing a shape beside it—a bent man, hunched and silent, holding a spade and bowing his head.

The maintenance crew tried to cut it down. The first swing of the axe echoed through the grounds—followed by a low, guttural wailing from deep inside the trunk.

They tried fire. Old Book appeared in the smoke, hovering near the flames, his outline barely visible, his grief undiminished. The flames sputtered and died.

Nothing would kill the tree—until nature took matters into its own hands. One summer, a bolt of lightning struck the elm and split it in two. The Crying Tree finally fell onto the edge of the potter's field where the nameless and the unwanted had been buried.

But even in death, some things linger.

The Mourner Still Walks

They say if you wander the old grounds on a damp morning—fog curls low and still—you might see a man in faded hospital garb leaning against an invisible trunk, his shoulders rising and falling with the weight of some eternal, wordless sorrow.

He doesn't speak. He never did.

But you'll feel it in your bones:

Not all the ghosts in Bartonville scream.

Some just mourn.

Forever.

Indiana: Big Tunnel—The Dancing Dead Light

The Belly of the Beast

The Big Tunnel between Fort Ritner and Tunnelton is no mere relic of the railroad age—it is a living thing, a beast made of stone and soot. It yawns across the land like the open mouth of something waiting to feed. What it swallows, it keeps.

The tunnel was carved through solid rock in 1857, a marvel of the Ohio and Mississippi Railway's ambition.

Later lined with bricks and dark intentions, it stretches beneath the land like an artery cut deep through the limestone hills of Lawrence County, Indiana. It is cold in there, even in high summer, and damp as a grave. Locals say the walls drip with more than water. It oozes with death. They say the tunnel is seeped with memories of a murder that won't go away.

A Mysterious Death

For over a century, people have whispered of strange lights that drift just beyond the reach of day, footsteps with no source for the sound, and shadows that cling too close. However, one story rooted in fact still chills the town of Tunnelton to this day—the death of night watchman Henry Dixon.

It happened in the early hours of Thursday, July 23, 1908, when the man assigned to the daytime shift arrived at the tunnel to relieve his night counterpart. He expected to find 27-year-old Henry Dixon inside the small watchman's shack near the east portal, perhaps smoking or dozing lightly after the long shift.

Instead, the shack was empty.

The silence around it was unnatural—not the soft silence of early morning, but something taut and observant. The day man called out. Nothing.

Then, from the black maw of the tunnel, he saw it: the glow of a lantern, faint and flickering like a candle too far gone to hold its flame. He stepped into the tunnel. And the tunnel swallowed him. Roughly two hundred feet in, he found Dixon's body. It lay crumpled on the gravel beside the tracks, limp and already cold.

Blood matted his dark hair. A deep wound had torn into the left side of his skull, the force of it cracking bone like dry kindling. Nearby lay two lanterns—one still lit, the other shattered. His cap had been flung nearly forty feet away. His pockets had been turned out and emptied.

It was not a death by accident.

It was blunt, intimate violence.

The Mystery Deepens

Henry Dixon had been a familiar figure in Tunnelton. Quiet, punctual, and respected for his work, he was responsible for walking the tunnel before each train passed through, checking for fallen debris or track damage. His signal lantern told approaching engineers whether the path was safe. That morning, around 4:00 a.m., Train No. 12—an express passenger route from St. Louis to Cincinnati—entered the Big Tunnel.

It should have been halted. No clearance had been given. And yet, the engineer reported that he had seen a man. He described a figure inside the tunnel holding two lanterns, standing off to the side. The figure made no signal. It stood still and watched the train pass.

When the engineer turned to look again, the figure was gone.

Days earlier, Dixon had aided two young women who sought to walk through the tunnel but were heckled by a group of local men. After Dixon safely escorted them through, a confrontation followed. Words escalated. One man, red-faced and reeking of whiskey, reportedly told Dixon, *"If I catch you alone in that tunnel, one of us is coming out dead."*

The threat was remembered but never proven.

No charges were brought. No confessions were made. And the brick-lined throat of the Big Tunnel kept its secrets. Dixon was laid to rest in Proctor Cemetery, a stone's throw from where he died.

But the living say he never truly left.

The Dancing Light

Sometimes, a couple of lights dance deep within the tunnel. Sometimes one. It hovers just beyond reach, gently bobbing like it's being carried by an unseen hand. Witnesses have followed it, thinking it a vagrant or a prank. But the light doesn't respond. It doesn't waver. It simply vanishes.

Those who've seen it swear it resembles the dual lanterns Dixon was known to carry. A silent warning. Or a replay of his final moments. Some even claim the ghost can be seen just off the tracks, head bowed, hand outstretched, forever caught in the act of signaling a train that will never stop.

It Feeds on the Living

The tunnel remains open today, though few dare to linger inside. Its brick walls are damp, its shadows too dense, and the silence inside too absolute—broken only by the occasional drip, the groan of old stone, or the sharp, metallic ring of something that shouldn't move in the dark. If you see a light there—*don't follow*. It goes deeper and deeper into its gaping jaws, leading those who follow into its darkness and drawing them in. Chewing them up. Never spitting them out.

Because the Big Tunnel remembers. And it feeds.

Indiana: The Dark Weeper in the Woods—Stepp Cemetery

A Place Meant to Be Forgotten

Hidden deep within the folds of Morgan-Monroe State Forest, just north of Martinsville, Indiana, lies one of the oldest cemeteries in the state. Stepp Cemetery sits quietly among the trees, nearly swallowed by them—only a simple iron gate and a scattering of aging stones marking its existence.

It is not a place one stumbles upon. You must go looking for it. And even then, the woods seem to close in behind you.

Established in the early 1800s, the cemetery once served the sparse settlers of Monroe and Morgan Counties. Generations came and went. Children were buried before their parents. Entire families faded into moss and soil.

Time moved on. But something stayed.

The Mourner in the Shadows

According to decades of witness accounts, a woman in black still walks the far edge of the cemetery near a small, weather-worn grave believed to belong to an infant. Always veiled, always dressed in mourning, she kneels over the child's resting place—sometimes silently rocking.

Other times, weeping.

And there are nights when it's said she digs.

She pulls at the dirt with bare, slow hands as if trying to unearth the child again.

Not to disturb. Not to desecrate. But to hold.

Witnesses claim that once the child is in her arms—a tiny bundle of cloth, bones, and memory—she retreats to a rotting stump near the tree line. She sits, swaying gently back and forth, the baby cradled to her chest. Approach her, and she disappears into the woods without a sound. Wait long enough, and you may hear the sobbing start again—soft at first, then circling through the trees like wind caught in a scream.

The Sect That Stirred the Soil

By the mid-20th century, the cemetery's isolation began to attract curious teenagers.

Bonfires. Dares.

Midnight rituals of their own invention.

The graveyard became a whispered legend passed through generations; its silence disturbed by those who sought fear but didn't understand it.

But long before these revelers ever arrived, a different kind of gathering took place among the stones.

In the early 1900s, Stepp Cemetery was frequented by a fringe religious sect known as the Crabbites—a group led by William Crabb, known for practices considered bizarre even by the standards of early Pentecostal movements.

Snake-handling.

Trances.

Spiritual possession.

And, if some reports are to be believed, the ritual calling of the dead.

The Crabbites were never officially linked to crimes. But they left something behind. Something unseen.

A residue.

A current in the air that makes the hairs on your neck rise before you even reach the gate.

Some locals claim the sect's final rites were never completed.

Others say the ghostly woman is one of their own, lost in a grief ritual that spiraled into madness.

The Sounds No One Can Trace

Even on the clearest nights, Stepp Cemetery does not feel open. There's something about the tree line—too tight, too dark.

Visitors report hearing soft chanting. A rhythmic, low hum that rolls just beneath the rustle of leaves.

Others have heard weeping.

Some describe howls. Occasionally, a voice calls out by name.

There are no lights. No nearby houses. And once you're deep in the dark forest, cell reception vanishes entirely. If you hear crying, you will not find the source. If you see a figure kneeling near a grave—do not speak.

And if she turns to look at you, *do not run*.

She only follows those who try to leave.

Iowa: The Black Angel of Oakland Cemetery

The Statue That Turned Dark

An angel stands in the quiet heart of Iowa City, nestled within the weathered gates of Oakland Cemetery.

She is not the radiant figure one might expect in a place of mourning. Her once golden bronze wings are now cloaked in a midnight hue. Her head bows low—not in grace, but in sorrow.

In warning. In grief so deep it seems to bend the stone.

They call her The Black Angel.

She was placed there by Teresa F. McGowan, a woman who had already lost too much. Her only child, Edward, died at the age of eighteen from meningitis. A boy full of promise reduced to silence in less than a week.

The angel was her final gesture. Her final prayer.

And possibly… her final spell.

The Mother, the Monument, the Mourning

Teresa did not choose the angel's pose by accident. She commissioned a statue that would tilt its head downward—eternally watching Edward's grave at her feet. Beneath the statue, his resting place is marked by a peculiar monument: the lower trunk of a tree, its top blown clean off. Cut short. Life ended too soon.

They say Teresa had the angel cast in gold bronze. But even in its first days, the metal began to darken. Oxidation, some say. Others believe Teresa meant it that way. That she knew something was coming for him. She called down protection—not only for her son's soul but for the sacred silence that surrounded his grave.

Because she knew others would come.

And not all would come with kindness.

Beware: She Watches Over Him

Time passed. Teresa died. But the angel remained. Her arms stretched down. Her wings curved wide. Her eyes—though stone—seemed always watching.

And something else began.

Visitors began to whisper of unease.

A coldness that clung to them even in high summer.

The sensation of being watched. Touched. Pulled.

Whispers curled from behind gravestones. Strange lights blinked through the trees. Shadowy forms passed between rows of the dead, moving too quickly—and vanishing too easily.

Those with ill intent, pranksters, vandals, those who mocked the angel—did not stay long. Some say the air itself repels them. Others speak of mechanical failures, sudden illness, or nightmares that followed them home.

Those Who Legend Trip

And then came the legends.

Folklore took root in the cemetery soil, passed through high school corridors and campfires alike:

If a virgin kisses someone before the Black Angel, her darkness will lift, and her bronze will return.

Touch her at midnight on Halloween, and you'll die within seven years.

Kiss the angel herself, and you die on the spot.

No one knows where the stories began. No one knows if they are warnings or temptations. But still—they circulate. Still, people test them.

Still, the angel watches.

Those Who Dare Pay the Price

Not so long ago, three teenagers visited the grave.

They came to prove it was all just shadowplay.

Cheap legend. Rusted bronze and dead stories.

But they didn't stay long.

They claimed something surrounded them—an invisible pressure, like air folding inward.

They saw lights—not flashlights, not fireflies but soft, blue flickers that danced in the trees without heat or source. The forest had no wind, yet the leaves rustled.

One girl began to cry. Not from fear, she said. From despair. A grief she didn't recognize but felt so deeply it stole her breath.

They left before midnight.

They did not go back. They never, ever went back.

In the end, it is not the statue that frightens most.

It is the feeling that someone is standing behind you when you approach it.

Watching.

Waiting.

Judging.

And perhaps... remembering who you are.

So it can follow you in your worst nightmares.

Iowa: The Hollow Where Pearl Waits—The Mossy Glen Murders

Blood in the Basket

They say the land never forgot what happened at Mossy Glen. That the ground drank too deeply, and something in the trees learned how to whisper. The story begins in 1936, when 27-year-old Pearl Hines Shine, a red-haired bride of just six days, helped orchestrate the brutal murder of her husband, Dan Shine—a 58-year-old farmer who worked 80 acres of rugged, isolated land in the dark folds of the hollow.

She didn't act alone.

Her lover, Maynard Lenox, a gangly harmonica-playing 18-year-old, and a junk dealer named Deke Cornwell, carried out the killing. Pearl's parents, Jim and Minnie Hines, also had a hand in the scheme. Minnie was the mother of 18 children.

But the child she cared most about was Pearl.

And on that day, Pearl wanted blood.

How to Kill a Husband

It began with a blow.

Lenox struck Dan Shine hard, shoving him backward into the dirt. Then Cornwell brought a full beer bottle down onto Dan's skull. It didn't shatter—just caved in bone with a sickening, wet crunch.

Still breathing, Dan was dragged up the staircase of his home like a sack of spoiled meat. Blood pooled beneath him, seeping into the wooden planks as they stuffed him into the upstairs closet. Then, with a rifle aimed point-blank, Lenox pulled the trigger.

The blast ripped away half of Dan Shine's face.

His jaw disintegrated. His cheekbone exploded. Pieces of him sprayed across the wall, the ceiling, and the closet door, where flecks of his hair clung to drying blood.

They weren't done. They stuffed the body into a clothes basket. They ran a string from his hand to the rifle trigger to stage a suicide—a lie so lazy it could only come from people who thought the dead were beneath suspicion.

But the sheriff didn't buy it. Neither did his wife.

Why I Killed My Husband

When the sheriff sent his wife to retrieve clothes for Pearl in jail, she found a small travel bag.

Inside: underthings, a comb, and a romance magazine. A dog-eared page caught her eye. The title? "Why I Killed My Husband."

It was as if Pearl had left behind a signed confession hidden between perfume samples and fashion tips.

Dan Shine was buried quickly but not quietly. His coffin went into the earth beneath a sky thick with storm clouds.

No flowers. No mourning. Only silence and thunder.

Pearl was sentenced to the Rockwell City Women's Reformatory. Maynard Lenox was locked away in the Fort Madison State Penitentiary. Deke Cornwell disappeared into the system like trash thrown in a river.

But the dead didn't go away.

And neither did the Hollow.

The Thing That Stirs in Mossy Glen

Mossy Glen Hollow lies just outside Strawberry Point, Iowa. A place of wild springs, jutting rock, and trees so dense they knit the light into shadows.

The forest is beautiful. Unspoiled. But *wrong*.

People say the air there feels thick. Old. Used.

And if you follow the old game trail toward where Dan Shine's house once stood, you'll see it: a dark patch where nothing grows.

Where branches bow inward. Where birds fall silent.

That's where they see her.

Pearl. Her red hair turned gray by time and fire. Her dress always wet with blood at the hem. Sometimes, she's crouched near the edge of the box canyon, rocking back and forth, whispering things only the trees hear. Other times, she stands with her head thrown back, screaming.

Not for forgiveness. Not for mercy.

But because she's still here.

The Ghost Who Screams With Her

But Pearl is not alone.

Years before Dan's murder, a traveling peddler made his way through Mossy Glen, selling buttons, needles, and spices to homesteads too far from town. During a desperate winter, a group of men robbed him, killed him, and buried his body in a cave so cold it preserved his flesh longer than it should have.

They say you can still hear him, especially in late autumn. A hollow moaning that rises and falls like wind—but with a sound too human to be wind.

And here's the curse: Pearl cannot escape him.

The peddler's voice follows her in death, just as surely as guilt did in life. Some say it's part of her punishment—that Hell, for Pearl Shine, is forever listening to that wail.

She cannot silence it. She cannot outrun it.

She can only endure it. As we endure her.

Mossy Glen looks peaceful at a distance. But step beneath the canopy, and the woods close in like a throat.

Somewhere inside, Pearl is still trying to forget what she did. And the Hollow refuses to let her.

Kansas: Dead Man in the Hollow— The Lost Name of Mallow

A Cabin at the Edge

In the earliest days of Atchison's founding, long before the cemetery fences and train tracks framed the modern town, a man named Mallow lived at the rim of a steep ravine. His homestead perched above the Missouri River, on land just east of where Jackson Park's wetlands now murmur beneath overgrowth.

Mallow was a trapper and fur trader.

Reclusive. Weathered.

He spoke little, worked alone, and operated a modest ferry in the 1850s. Though it stood in the shadow of the larger and more prosperous George Million ferry just upstream, Mallow's operation provided a quieter, rougher crossing for westward-bound settlers—ten to twelve wagons at a time, their livestock kicking dust as they gathered near his campfire.

For many of these families, his patch of land was a place of rest before they vanished westward into uncertain territory and tribal lands.

A night spent in Mallow's clearing meant a day spared from ambush, isolation, or starvation. And so they came, hundreds of them.

He guided them across and returned in silence.

And then—he was gone. Vanished.

The Hollow Begins to Whisper

In the late 1850s, without farewell or trace, Mallow vanished. Some believed he wandered off, felled by illness or accident in the isolated pocket of woodlands.

Others whispered darker things: something pulled him beneath the water he once navigated, or his silence had masked sins that came calling in the night.

His ferry never ran again. His cabin rotted slowly into the hillside. And the hollow began to change.

Reports trickled in—of flickering lights, of footsteps where none should tread, and of moaning that rose with the river fog. Mallow's clearing was abandoned, and the surrounding ravine became a known place of ripe fear.

By the Civil War, the hollow had been largely forsaken—except by outlaws and raiders, who found comfort in its shelter. Confederate bushwhackers reportedly camped in its shadowed arms, licking wounds and sharpening knives. They said it was the only place in Atchison where the dead outnumbered the living.

From Mallow to Molly

Over time, memory became distorted.

By the 1880s, as language softened and the original story faded, "Mallow's Hollow" became "Molly's Hollow"—a shift born of mispronunciation and the town's growing detachment from its frontier past.

The name stuck. The stories changed.

By the 1950s, Jackson Park was a magnet for local teens, who strolled up the old rail lines from Third and Main. They passed beneath rustling trees and into the valley where the old ferry grounds had been. Whispers followed them. Stories of high-pitched screams. Of fleeting shadows.

Of figures slipping between branches just out of reach.

Few remembered Mallow. Instead, they spoke of Molly—a girl who lived in a lone cabin deep in the woods. They said she was murdered there. That her cries still echoed up through the trees. That her spirit had been strung up and left to hang in the same hollow that once ferried wagons across the Missouri. And there was more.

The Strap That Would Not Fall

In one version of the tale, it was not Molly who screamed—but a man who hanged himself in the hollow long before anyone had ever heard the name Molly at all.

They say he used a leather strap knotted around a low tree limb. He was bloated and gray when they found him. The man was swaying gently above the earth.

His body was taken down, but the strap was not.

Children would hike to the swimming hole that later formed in the glen and see the strap still hanging, weathered and fraying, yet never gone. It stayed there for years. For decades. Maybe still.

The land kept its own calendar. It did not forget.

Screams from the Wrong Ghost

Today, curious visitors venture into Jackson Park hoping to see the ghost of Molly. They walk the looping trails and point at trees.

They wait for her cry.

Some say they hear it—a sharp, stuttering scream that echoes once, then fades.

Others report shadows, long and thin, flitting near the roots.

But those who know the story's beginning know better.

That scream does not belong to *Molly*.

It belongs to *Mallow*, the man who lived alone above the ravine. The man who ferried the desperate across the river then disappeared without witness or grave—the man who now screams—both in vengeance but also in frustration.

Because his name has been taken.

And no one is listening.

Kansas: Blue Light Lady—Fort Hays

She Gave Her Life for the Dying

They called her Elizabeth Polly in life—a kind hospital matron who walked the plague-ridden halls of Fort Hays during the summer of 1867. She was young, resolute, and unflinching in the face of death. When cholera swept through the fort like a black wind, Elizabeth refused to leave. She stayed behind to care for the infected, even as the disease claimed them one by one.

Then, it claimed her.

With no fanfare, no funeral procession, she was buried quietly in a blue dress and white bonnet near the edge of Sentinel Hill, her grave unmarked. A silent resting place. A final kindness denied.

But Elizabeth Polly did not rest.

She Walks the Hill Still

Not long after her burial, rumors began to rise like mist off the prairie. Travelers passing Sentinel Hill at dusk began to report an eerie, blue light floating just above the ground—flickering like fire behind a curtain of fog.

Some called it a lantern.

Others claimed it pulsed like a heartbeat.

And sometimes, that light had a face.

Witnesses began describing a woman in a tattered prairie dress drifting silently across the crest of the hill. She did not walk but glided—her movements mournful, her figure pale. Her face was hidden behind the veil of twilight, but her anguish clung to the trees like frost.

They called her The Blue Light Lady.

Soon, they stopped walking down the hill after dark.

The Lantern That Takes

There are tales whispered even now—low and urgent—of the Blue Lady's lantern and what happens if you meet her gaze.

Some say the light within it is not fire but something far older and hungrier.

To look directly into it is to feel your soul tug at the edges, like fabric caught on thorns.

A long enough stare can steal the breath from your lungs, replacing it with silence. Those who peer too long into her lantern have become lost.

Not missing. Not dead. Simply… gone.

No sound. No scent. No trace.

Only the light moving further away.

The Officer Who Hit the Dead

One of the most unnerving accounts comes from 1950. A police officer patrolling near Sentinel Hill in the early hours reported striking a woman in blue.

The impact was sharp.

Sudden.

He skidded to a halt and bolted from his cruiser, expecting to find a broken body in the road.

But there was nothing.

No one. No blood. No torn fabric.

Only a heavy stillness pressed against his skin like a damp cloth.

His flashlight refused to pierce the dark. He only saw a faint shimmer of blue, hovering briefly at the edge of the hill… before vanishing altogether.

He radioed it in. They searched. Found nothing.

But the officer never drove that road again.

No Grave to Hold Her

Elizabeth Polly's final resting place has never been found. Her grave remains unmarked. Some say that's why she can't rest—that a soul buried without a name can never be remembered properly.

The forgotten are always the most dangerous.

Others claim she walks not out of grief but out of punishment—cursed to retrace the same paths she walked while alive, carrying light for those she once tried to save, only to lead the living into the same shadows that consumed her.

And still, the hill waits.

If you hear the wind shift at dusk near Fort Hays—if the sky bruises violet and you see a faint blue glow where none should be—turn away.

Do not follow. Do not look for her face.

Because if Elizabeth Polly sees you first, her light will find you.

And you will not come back.

Kentucky: Headless Horror of Fort Thomas

A Journey into Darkness

She was 22, devout, and well-loved—Pearl Bryan, a Sunday School teacher from Greencastle, Indiana. Her smile was known by all in town, but her secret belonged to only one: Scott Jackson, a dental student in Cincinnati and the man who had left her five months pregnant.

In January 1896, she told her family she was visiting friends in Indianapolis.

She was not.

Pearl crossed state lines to seek out Jackson, clinging to the promise he would "take care of it."

Jackson, along with his cold-eyed roommate Alonzo Walling, had no intention of kindness. They offered her a backroom remedy—a makeshift abortion. What happened instead was a calculated descent into brutality.

They lured her to a saloon. She was drugged with cocaine, dazed, her vision swimming.

And then, when she was too weak to resist, they led her into the night.

A Gruesome Discovery

On the morning of February 1, 1896, a 17-year-old farmhand named Johnny Hewling stumbled upon a horror along the outskirts of Fort Thomas, Kentucky. There, in the frozen mud, a woman's body lay crumpled at the base of a ditch.

She was still clothed. Her arms folded strangely.

And her head—gone.

Not severed cleanly. Torn. Ripped.

Mutilated with grotesque force.

The soil was slick with darkened blood that had already begun to stiffen in the frost.

It was the shoes that told her name—custom-made, ordered in Greencastle. The only part of Pearl Bryan they couldn't strip away.

The coroner's report confirmed the unthinkable: she had still been alive when they began cutting.

Her windpipe was severed as she struggled.

She choked to death in silence.

Her head has never been recovered.

Justice, if it Can Be Called That

Scott Jackson and Alonzo Walling were quickly arrested, their lies unraveling under the weight of public fury. Both men remained eerily calm in jail, showing no remorse.

Rumors swirled that they had offered Pearl's head to a Satanic group.

Others claimed they buried it under a Cincinnati slaughterhouse.

The truth was never found.

The pair were kept under heavy guard, fearing a lynch mob. Even during a mass jailbreak, they did not flee—as if they knew hell was waiting either way.

On March 20, 1897, before a throng of thousands, both men were hanged side by side in Newport, Kentucky. Their necks snapped quickly.

But the silence that followed did not last.

That was the last public hanging in Campbell County.

It is said the wind screamed louder than the crowd.

An Enduring Haunting

But justice did not lay Pearl Bryan to rest.

Reports began to emerge within weeks. A woman in white drifting along the ravine where her body had been discarded. But her face was never seen. Because she has none. She walks Fort Thomas still, tethered to the land that drank her blood.

Her form is seen most often in the moments before dawn—gliding through the mist, arms stretched as if reaching, always reaching, for something just out of sight.

Some say she searches for her lost child. Others believe she is hunting for her head—and for the men who took it.

And some, those who speak only in whispers, say she does not walk alone. That on certain nights, two shadowy figures trail behind her—dragging something heavy through the underbrush.

If you walk the edge of Fort Thomas after dark, and you hear soft footsteps where no one walks, do not turn around.

If you hear your name spoken low and wet, do not answer.

For Pearl Bryan is still searching.

And she has not yet forgiven.

Kentucky: Ghost Dog with a Bone to Pick

A Town Drowned and Forgotten

Before the lake came, before the Tennessee Valley Authority swallowed the land for recreation and flood control, there was a place called Golden Pond. Nestled along Elbow Creek, it was a rough little town—full of moonshine, blood feuds, and hard men with harder habits. During Prohibition, it was known more for its liquor stills than anything golden.

Fights were frequent, disappearances accepted, and the law stayed far enough away to avoid trouble.

Today, Golden Pond lies mostly beneath the surface of Land Between the Lakes, forgotten by maps and scrubbed from memory.

But something still stirs there.

The Murder in the Woods

In the late 1920s, Paul Jackson was a familiar face in town—a wiry man with a sharp tongue and a devoted companion: an old hound dog that never left his side. They were seen together at every still, every poker table, every fight.

One humid summer night, Jackson sat down for cards with Ned Crawford, a man known for his short fuse and cold eyes. The cabin was deep in the woods, the windows shut tight, and the stakes were high.

The argument began over a hand of spades. Accusations flew. Then chairs.

Crawford plunged a knife into Jackson's chest. Once. Twice. A third time for good measure.

As Jackson hit the floor, his dog howled like a soul being ripped in two and lunged for Crawford's throat. The animal sank its teeth in deep, but it was no match for Crawford's blade.

The hound was butchered on the cabin floor.

Crawford dragged both bodies to the nearest pond—black, still water that reflected nothing—and dumped them like garbage. He walked away, leaving blood on the porch and boot prints in the mud.

The Dog That Would Not Die

That night, as Crawford returned to his cabin, something moved at the edge of the tree line.

A shape. Low to the ground. Silent.

Then—a growl.

When he turned, he saw it: the dog, wet and caked in mud, standing where the moonlight couldn't reach. Its eyes glowed white. Its teeth were bared.

It did not bark. It did not lunge.

It simply watched.

And from that moment on, it never stopped watching.

Wherever Crawford went—to the outhouse, store, and creek—the dog was there, waiting in the dark. It appeared in the corners of rooms, behind trees, in the fog just outside the door. It left no tracks. Made no sound.

But it growled.

The Haunting of Ned Crawford

The law never came for Crawford. He buried his guilt beneath liquor and moved on like nothing happened.

But the dog didn't.

Crawford's health began to rot. He stopped sleeping. Couldn't eat. He saw eyes in every window and heard growls behind every wall.

He fled the state.

Still, the hound followed.

It showed up at his boarding house in Nashville. In the alley behind a butcher shop in Memphis. It waited outside a tent revival in Mississippi. Wherever he went, so did the ghost with white eyes and blood-stiffened fur.

Eventually, broken and barely able to stand, Crawford crawled back to Kentucky.

The Bone in the Hound's Mouth

A kind-hearted farmer took pity and gave him work. But Crawford was a shell—his hands trembled, his teeth chattered, his eyes never stopped darting to the shadows.

Then, one moonless night, walking down an old road near the lake, the farmer and Crawford came upon a shape beside the water. A massive black hound. Still. Silent. And in its jaws—a yellowed human leg bone.

The farmer later said Crawford screamed like a man being flayed alive. He fell to his knees, crying, begging, confessing to everything. He named the cabin. The knife. The pond. The bone. They arrested him the next day.

The Hound Remains

The town of Golden Pond is gone now, drowned beneath still water and tangled roots. But the dog remains. Its howl echoes on moonless nights—low and drawn out, like a sound from another world. Campers near Land Between the Lakes have reported growls outside their tents. Fishermen have seen ripples with no wind. Rangers have found pawprints that vanish at the edge of the lake. They say the dog is still looking. Still guarding. And if you listen—really listen—you might hear it behind you.

Just… there.

Don't turn around.

It's not barking. It's watching.

If you've got something to confess—now is the time.

Louisiana: The Storm Julia Sang—Frenier Louisiana

Built Between the River and the Dead

The town of Frenier should never have been built. Wedged between the Mississippi River and Lake Pontchartrain, the narrow strip of land was more swamp than soil. The trees were the first to go—felled by loggers who sent barge after barge of cypress and pine to New Orleans. Then came cabbage farming. Black, fertile ground that yielded endless rows of crops for sauerkraut.

But nothing grows there now. The water took it back.

And it may have taken more than just the land.

The Woman with One Foot in the Grave

Julia Brown had lived in Frenier for decades by the time the soil began to sour. She was a traiteur, a healer of old ways. Part Catholic, part conjure woman, part midwife. She knew herbs, bones, and the right kind of silence. People came to her with aches, fevers, and curses.

And she answered them in whispers.

After her husband Celestin died, Julia rarely left her porch. Those who passed would see her in her rocking chair, eyes unfocused, lips murmuring strange verses. She made up songs—soft and strange lullabies.

One in particular caught the ears of the children: "When I die, I'll take half of Frenier with me."

They laughed. Nervously. She didn't.

The Coffin Box and the Hurricane

Julia Brown died on September 28, 1915. By the afternoon, the mourners came—neighbors, family, and friends. They filed past the pine coffin box in her parlor, some clutching rosaries, others only memories. The storm, they said, was coming—but they had seen storms before.

They weren't afraid.

They should have been.

By 4:00 p.m., the sky burst open, spewing down rain and retching out wind. The New Orleans hurricane had arrived with no mercy. The rain gushed like a flood. Windows blew inward. Doors ripped from hinges.

And the water came fast—black, heaving, and full of debris.

People scrambled to tables. Then to rafters. Then to rooftops.

And then into the dark.

Dragged Into the Swamp

The screams came next.

Mothers clutching infants were torn from rooftops and pulled under like weeds. Couples clawed for one another in the floodwaters before vanishing beneath floating barrels, lumber, and corpses.

One man survived by clinging to a tree. He shoved his hands to his ears to block out the sound of people drowning.

They found the bodies later.

Children caught in the crooks of trees.

Old men crushed beneath house beams.

One woman was impaled by a fencepost that had sailed through the air like a javelin.

The casket was gone. So was Julia.

Her Song, Her Curse

Later, they found it.

The coffin box bobbing near the edge of the swamp split open. Julia's body had washed far from it, tangled in reeds like something discarded. She was smiling, they said. Or maybe the skin had stretched in death.

Some said she had warned them.

Others said she had called the storm herself.

The hurricane killed at least 28 people in Frenier alone.

All that remained was a graveyard and ruins choked by cypress moss. And somewhere beneath the lakebed, the bones of a healer who had sung a promise.

"When I die, I'll take half of Frenier with me."

What Was Left Behind

The storm drowned the town, but it didn't end the story.

Fishermen hear strange melodies drifting across the water.

Tourists say the swamp whispers at dusk.

And those who stray too close to Frenier's forgotten edge swear they see a woman on the water—rocking, softly humming, eyes closed.

No one goes looking for Julia Brown.

They say she sings still.

And that her voice carries storms.

If the wind dies and the lake lies still, listen closely. You may hear a song you weren't meant to hear.

And if you do… start running.

'Cause Julia Brown will take you with her.

Louisiana: Moaning Mona Lisa Smiles—City Park, New Orleans

The Statue with a Secret Face

At the turn of the twentieth century, a grieving father gave a gift to the city of New Orleans: a series of elegant and classical bronze statues positioned near what is now known as Popp's Fountain in City Park. Each figure was a tribute to beauty, to memory, to culture.

But one statue stood apart from the others. She was cast in the form of Venus, the Roman goddess of love.

And if you looked closely, the face was not idealized marble perfection. It bore the soft, knowing expression of a real girl.

The slight parting of the lips.

The tilt of the chin.

The unmistakable, ghostly echo of a Mona Lisa smile.

The girl was the man's daughter. She had drowned in one of the park's lagoons—not by accident, but by sorrow.

A Love That Was Forbidden

She had fallen for a sailor—a man of the sea, wild and strange, who came ashore with storms in his eyes and brine on his skin. He was not from their world. Her father forbade it. He was not a man to be crossed.

So, she did not run away. She did not fight. She simply walked—silent and graceful as a statue—into the green-black water of the lagoon.

They said she never screamed.

And her body was found with that same Mona Lisa smile still frozen on her lips.

The statue came after. It was a lie shaped in bronze.

Where Lovers Park and Spirits Wake

Time passed. The statue weathered. The polished skin of Venus turned dark with oxidation. Moss clung to her legs. Her once-smooth hands began to crack. The water rose and fell. The girl was all but forgotten. But the statue never stopped smiling. By the mid-century, the cul-de-sac where the pathway ended had become a lover's lane, hidden by trees and thick humidity.

Teenagers parked their cars there. They whispered the story of the statue in half-truths and urban legend, laughing nervously as fog crept in from the lagoon.

Until one night—a car, too fast, too loud, spun off the road and slammed into the statue.

The bronze woman cracked and fell.

That's when the stories changed.

She Scratches the Glass

Soon after, couples parked in the area reported a figure rising from the pond.

Not fully formed.

Not flesh. Not mist.

Something between. A girl soaked and moaning, her hands dragging slowly across the earth.

Some said she moved like she was underwater, even on land—her limbs drifting unnaturally, head tilted, mouth still curled in that same eerie smile. She appeared beside car windows, leaving wet prints on the glass and long, shallow scratches that didn't stop at the paint.

One boy said her face was pressed to the window, eyes wide and unfocused.

When he blinked, she was gone—but the glass was smeared with lake water and something like blood.

Another girl swore she saw the ghost in the rearview mirror—sitting silently in the back seat, hands folded in her lap, smiling as if waiting to be driven home.

They Took the Statue—But Not the Spirit

Eventually, the statue was vandalized beyond repair.

It was removed. But the girl remained.

She has been heard wailing across the water in the early hours before dawn. She has been seen gliding silently along the edge of the lagoon, pale feet not quite touching the ground.

She doesn't speak.

She doesn't scream.

She only moans.

And the Mona Lisa smile never leaves her face.

They say if you sit alone at Popp's Fountain in the dark, you'll hear the soft scrape of her nails on the concrete nearby.

And if you dare look over your shoulder, you may find her smiling at you.

Because love drowned once here—

and left something behind.

Maine: The Devil's Footprint—North Manchester Meeting House

The Devil's Footprint

The North Manchester Meeting House is tucked into the folds of the Maine countryside, surrounded by stoic woods and weathered fields. Raised in 1793, its timber frame and hand-forged hinges have held fast through centuries of storms, sermons, and silence. A small burial ground is not far from its shadow, hemmed in by a crumbling stone wall. The air there is still—not peaceful, but suspended as though the ground itself is listening.

Visitors speak in hushed tones when they walk the edge of that wall. Not out of reverence but out of caution. Because in one corner, near where the tree roots claw their way through the stones, something remains.

Three impressions.

Not quite footprints. But not quite anything else.

One is shaped like a cloven hoof.

The Stone That Would Not Move

The legend begins during the wall's construction. Masons and farmers alike had gathered to raise the boundary with fieldstone—pulling boulders from the hills, setting them in dry-stacked rows to mark the edge of the consecrated land.

But one stone wouldn't budge.

No team of oxen, no lever or rope could loosen it. It sat defiant, unmoving and cold. Day after day, the workers struggled. Tempers flared. Until one man snapped.

In a moment of frustration, he shouted what he should never have said: "I'd sell my soul to the devil if it meant getting this damn rock out of the ground."

The others laughed nervously, spat on the soil, and cursed him for tempting fate.

But the next morning, the boulder was gone.

And so was the man.

Three Marks and a Warning

They searched for him in the woods, by the rivers, in the root cellars of old farms. But he had vanished without a sound or sign—no boot prints, no belongings, no struggle.

Instead, they found three depressions in the corner of the wall, newly stamped into the stone itself.

One was long and narrow—like a man's bare foot.

The second was warped and bloated—misshapen like the skin had torn in the shaping of it.

The third, unmistakably, was a cloven hoof.

The masons would not touch that corner again.

They built around it.

And when the wall was finished, no one ever leaned against that stone. Not for rest. Not even to tie a bootlace.

Some said it pulsed with heat.

Others claimed it grew slick with frost, even in July.

Where the Pact Was Sealed

It's said the worker's soul was taken that night.

The devil had come not with fire but with the quiet inevitability of a contract honored.

Those who visit the graveyard today still find the three strange marks in the corner. The moss does not grow over them. Rain will not fill them. Even snow seems to melt around them in precise, unnatural shapes.

Some who come too close say they feel watched.

Others have felt something reach up, unseen, from beneath the earth—not to grab, but to… recognize.

If you visit North Manchester and feel drawn to the wall's far edge, walk slowly.

Look for the cloven mark in the stone.

And if you hear something whisper your name and ask if you need a favor granted—for God's sakes, do not answer.

Maine: Dark Shadows on Wood Island

Wood Island sits like a sentinel at the mouth of the Saco River—32 acres of wind-scarred brush and coastal stone, hemmed in by the gray breath of the Atlantic. Since 1807, its lighthouse has guided mariners away from the rocks, its white beacon sweeping across black water like a warning eye.

But long after the foghorn has gone silent and the beacon dims, the island remains alert. It remembers.

And it never forgets what happened there.

The Gentle Giant and the Strangers in the Coop

In the summer of 1896, Wood Island was quiet. Remote. Self-contained. Just off the coast of Biddeford Pool, it had its lighthouse, its keepers, and a single family trying to make a life where the land ends.

Fred Milliken was that man. A part-time sheriff, a game warden, and a father. They called him the Gentle Giant, a man of calm voice and even steadier hands. He lived on the island with his wife and three young children. Beside his family's cottage, Milliken owned a second structure—a converted chicken coop—which he rented to two young fishermen.

Howard Hobbs and William Moses, both 24, were rough around the edges but had no real history of trouble. Until they did.

Drunk and Drowning in the Past

In June 1896, Hobbs and Moses rowed to the mainland. They drank for two days—liquor mixed with salt air and something darker. When they returned to the island late that afternoon, their boat knocked softly against the shore. The wind had died. The sky was still.

Milliken met them on the path. Rent was overdue. He mentioned it gently, as he had many times before.

But Howard Hobbs didn't speak. He went into the shack, silent and shaking, and came out with a .42-caliber repeating rifle. The struggle was brief. A flash. A sound like the world tearing.

Milliken stumbled. His shirt bloomed red. His wife screamed as he fell to the dirt in front of her, hands clutching at his chest.

He died within forty-five minutes while his children stood nearby, screaming into the uncaring wind. Hobbs, trembling, ran to the lighthouse to call for help. But there was none left to give.

The Second Shot

Afterward, Hobbs returned to the chicken coop, now thick with the smell of gunpowder and something worse. He stepped inside. And he turned the rifle on himself.

They found him slumped in the corner, jaw shattered, blood pooled beneath the old floorboards, mixing with the dried feathers still clinging to the cracks in the wood.

The second man, William Moses, survived and never spoke of what Hobbs had said that night. The island went silent again. But only for a while.

What the Island Kept

Today, the lighthouse still stands. It is still bright, still watching. But those visiting the island say something else lingers beneath the light.

They hear muffled cries near the site of the old coop— like a man begging to be forgiven or a boy crying through clenched teeth.

In the tower, visitors speak of a shadowed figure watching them from above before vanishing. One woman swore she saw the shape of a man at the walkway's edge—but when she approached, he was gone, and the air was suddenly ice-cold.

Others have seen a woman's silhouette gliding soundlessly near the shoreline. She appears to float more than walk, always turning toward the sea, always just out of reach. A dead man's wife, looking for her husband.

The Children Still Cry

Some say the children's cries were the last thing the wind carried that day before it shifted. And that the lighthouse remembers their pitiful mewlings.

That the island listens to them.

When the fog rolls in and the tide pulls low, stand still near the lighthouse at Wood Island.

Stop.

Listen closely.

The air hangs heavy with the residue of the past, each sound soaked in sorrow and unrest, echoing with the unshakable weight of things long buried but never, ever truly gone.

Maryland: Unsettled Souls at Wise's Well

Where the Ground Refused the Dead

On September 14, 1862, the slopes of South Mountain ran red.

As the Union and Confederate armies clashed in the brutal Battle of South Mountain, the once-quiet valley of Fox's Gap became a crucible of cannon smoke, blood, and bone. The passes were strategic—gateways through which whole divisions could move. That made them prized. Fought for. Drenched.

At the center of this blood-soaked chessboard stood the Daniel Wise homestead, a modest farmstead where a father and his two children once tilled the soil. That soil—soon churned by musket fire and bootheels—would become a battlefield, then a field hospital, and finally, a mass graveyard for the mangled dead.

Where Shovels Broke on Stone

The Union Army prevailed. But victory brought no peace—only corpses. Thousands of them.

The occupying forces were tasked with the burial of the Confederate dead. Yet the ground—hard-packed, rocky, defiant—would not yield.

Men tried.

Shovels snapped.

The dirt allowed barely a foot and a half, barely enough to hide a ribcage. Fingers jutted through the soil like roots. Toes curled out of the earth, pale and stiff.

And then someone remembered the well.

The Drunken Butchers of Fox's Gap

Samuel W. Compton of the 12th Ohio Volunteer Infantry witnessed what followed: "On the morning of the 16th, I strolled out to see them bury the Confederate dead. I saw, but I never want to [see] another [such] sight. The squad I saw were armed with pick and canteen full of whiskey, the whiskey the most necessary of the two. The bodies had become so offensive that the men could only endure it by being staggering drunk. To see men stagger up to corpses and strike four or five times before they could get ahold, a right hold being one above the belt—"

They dragged them to the well and tumbled them in. A 60-foot drop.

A black pit of limbs and teeth and agony.

The smell was unbearable.

The sounds—wet, snapping, collapsing—worse.

Compton did not eat that night. Nor the next.

A Dollar for Every Soul

Daniel Wise was later paid a dollar per body dumped into his well. Not for compassion. Not for service. But, perhaps, as payment for ruining what had once been his family's water and his children's land.

Years passed before the Confederates' remains were exhumed and reinterred at Rose Hill Cemetery in Hagerstown. But by then, something had seeped into the stones, the soil, and the very grain of the farmhouse walls.

And it would not go quietly.

The Ghost Who Could Not Rest

When the Wise family returned to their land, the war was over—but another kind of siege began.

Each night, Daniel Wise was awakened by a presence—a soldier, half-shadow, standing above his bed. His lips did not move, but Daniel heard the words all the same:

"I am in an uncomfortable position. I cannot rest. You must bury me… properly."

The voice came again the next night.

And the next.

Until Daniel stopped sleeping.

The Well Still Moans

Today, the Wise homestead is gone. But the land remains scraped and scarred by time. Hikers along the Appalachian Trail, near the small pull-off along Reno Monument Road, sometimes pause and listen.

And what they hear is not the wind.

It is a thud, again and again—like bodies dropped from above, hitting the bottom of something hollow.

And sometimes, they hear more:

Moans.

Wet and low.

Full of suffering and soil.

They echo up from the place where the well once stood. They claw at the air and vanish before anyone can trace their source. But the ground remembers.

If you walk past Fox's Gap at dusk, listen closely.

The war is long over, but the dead still fall.

And moan.

And groan.

Wet and low.

Full of suffering and soil.

Some souls, buried in horror, do not forgive the living. Let us hope they do not follow you home. And stand over your bed, compelling you to move their unsettled spirits so they can finally rest.

Maryland: Stickpile Tunnel—Green Ridge Forest

From Orchard to Oblivion

Long before the trees returned, the land that would become Green Ridge Forest had already been stripped bare. In the 1800s, timbermen came first, slicing through the wilderness with saw and sweat. By the time the axes were silenced, the soil was raw—peeled like skin from bone. In 1870, the Mertens family bought up 32,000 acres of that desolate terrain and planted rows of apple trees, staking their future in green fruit and hard labor.

Their effort bore more than apples. A village grew alongside the orchard: Green Ridge Station, a collection of buildings anchored by canal lockkeepers, railway workers, and rough-hewn laborers.

There was a bunkhouse, a jelly factory, a post office, and the Mertens Saloon, where the orchardmen drank deep and fought louder. But fruit rots fast when fortunes fail. By 1920, the apples soured, the jelly factory shuttered, and the trees—once lined in perfect rows—gave way to weeds and wilderness. The town died. The forest returned.

But not everything stayed buried.

The Tunnel That Groaned

Carved into the earth like a black wound, the Green Ridge Tunnel stretched 1,705 feet through Maryland's belly. When the train came, the Mertens used it to ship apples far and wide. Its whistle shrieked through the valley like a war cry. And beneath the stone and steel, the darkness listened.

Sometime in those years—no one knows the exact date—a hobo tried to ride the rails through Green Ridge.

He didn't make it out.

They say his body was found inside the tunnel, crushed, twisted, and stained across the walls like a smear of rust and flesh. No name. No kin. Just a body. The men who found him didn't care much for ceremony. They dragged what remained into a corner of the tunnel and piled sticks over him like a heap of garbage as if bones could be forgotten with enough kindling. The tunnel took a new name after that—Stickpile Tunnel.

The Man Who Dances in Death

That should've been the end. But it wasn't. People walking near the tunnel—even today—speak of a figure rising from the stone floor. First, just a shadow. Then, a body that isn't quite a body. Limbs jerk at impossible angles. The head wobbles loose on the neck. And then he moves. He dances. But it's not a joyful dance. It's a grotesque, jerking marionette motion, as if unseen strings yank the corpse into a final, humiliating performance. His limbs snap. His back folds inward. His eyes—when they appear—glow dull like dying coals. Then he collapses. And vanishes.

Some hear a chuckle when he goes. Others hear crunching sticks. And one man, a rail worker who refused to enter the tunnel again, swore the ghost whispered in his ear: "Bury me right."

Where the Forest Watches

The town is gone. The orchard swallowed. What remains is moss-covered stone, tracks warped by time, and Stickpile Tunnel, gaping like a mouth waiting for another mistake. Those who walk the trail today say the air changes near the entrance. It grows dense. Hollow. Damp. Like breath too long held. And if you stay too long—if you look too closely—you might see movement just beyond the edge of light. A figure. Slouched. Waiting.

Stickpile Tunnel's entrances are now barred by heavy gates, but you can hike to it and peer within. If you feel something tug at your shoulder, don't turn around.

He's still there. Still dancing.

Still trying to crawl out from beneath the sticks.

Massachusetts: Pale Ghost of Boston Common

Born Among the Damned

In the choking heat of religious strife, Mary Dyer once walked proudly among the Puritans of 1630s Boston—until her thoughts, her womb, and her faith were all declared unclean.

She had come seeking God.

Instead, she found men who spoke for Him with sharpened tongues and rope in their hands.

The Monstrous Birth

On October 11, 1637, Mary gave birth to a child who did not live long enough to cry—a stillborn infant twisted by unknown deformities, born under candlelight and dread. The details were seized upon by Governor John Winthrop, who recorded the features in grotesque detail, calling the child monstrous—a sign, he said, that God had cursed her womb for heresy. She had merely followed her conscience.

They called her cursed.

But it was *their* religion that was based on twisted doctrines, dishonesty, and misguided beliefs.

Cast Out and Condemned

They turned her motherhood into a weapon. They dragged her grief into the public square, tearing her apart not for what she had done but for what she believed.

She fled—first to Rhode Island, then to England. And there, she found the Quakers—a faith of silence, light, and inner truth, where priests were unnecessary, and no one was above another in God's eyes. That belief—that God could be found without a pulpit—was enough to mark her for death.

She returned to Speak

1657 Mary returned to Massachusetts, knowing full well what awaited her. The Puritans had passed new laws: speak of Quaker beliefs, and you'd face prison. Return after banishment, and you would hang.

Mary Dyer came back anyway.

She came not to defy.

She came to warn. To warn that tyranny cloaked in holy words would rot every soul it touched.

That punishment born of pride was not justice—it was murder wrapped in scripture.

They arrested her.

She was hanged.

The rope bit her neck on a spring morning. And the wind, they say, was colder than it had ever been that time of year.

The White Woman of the Common

But Mary did not remain in the grave.

They buried her body. But not her message.

Soon after her death, people began to report strange things near Boston Common, the very ground she had passed through before her execution. A woman in white walking calmly through the morning fog. Her face turned down, her feet never touching the earth.

She carries no torch. No scripture. Only a presence.

Some say she is seen after arguments after violent words are spoken in the name of righteousness.

Some say she walks only when the city sleeps, her figure barely visible among the elm shadows—a warning, not a haunting.

Judgment Belongs to No Man

Witnesses have described the air growing colder in her wake. Whispers following behind, unintelligible but urgent. At times, the smell of damp linen. And always—always—that feeling that someone is watching. Judging. Remembering.

She is not angry.

She is disappointed.

"Let no man name God while he grips the throat of another," she once said.

And now, she walks to remind those who would forget. If you pass through Boston Common on a quiet night and feel your breath stall—do not speak.

You are in the company of Mary Dyer.

She died because others believed they were right.

She returns not only to show how wrong they were—but to reveal that the same quiet cruelties still fester beneath polished words and pious faces.

The very sins once cloaked in Puritan law may still be unfolding, right under our noses, in the guise of righteousness.

She walks among us to remind the living: the Puritans never truly left; they are just wearing different clothing and standing behind a different podium.

And they all will rot in Hell.

Michigan: Paulding Ghost Light

The Light That Waits in the Pines

Somewhere between the trees—where the road buckles and shadows twist—a light appears. It comes without warning.

Pale yellow. Flickering white.

Sometimes pulsing red. It hovers in the air, grows, shrinks, and dances like it knows you're watching.

And when it vanishes, the forest feels heavier, as though something has just passed through. Locals call it *The Paulding Light.* And it does not always wait to be seen.

The Couples Who Never Forgot

In 1966, four young couples drove together along Old Military Road, just past Dog Meadow. The sky was clear. The night was still. They killed their headlights, waiting in the dark for whatever they had heard whispered in town—a glow in the trees. A trick of the air. A ghost with nowhere left to go.

Then, without sound or warning, a blinding light flooded the car—bright enough to read by, cold as bone. It pierced the windows. It soaked the seats. It sat between them like something alive. They fled in a panic, tires screaming on gravel, and went straight to the sheriff.

But the light never left that place.

Built on Bone and Iron

Old Military Road was carved into the Upper Peninsula in the mid-1800s, following the mail routes and timber paths that had existed since the Civil War. It linked Fort Howard to Fort Wilkins, but more than soldiers used the trail. Miners. Traders. Deserters. Killers. All passed through those woods. Beneath the wagon wheels and sled tracks, the land remembered. And in time, the road became known not for the men who built it but for the things they left behind.

The Mailman Who Never Made It Home

The most enduring legend is not of war or riches but of silence. They say that in the dead of winter, a lone mail carrier ran his dogs across the path, delivering letters and parcels between frozen towns. The job was dangerous. Robbers were known to lie in wait, hidden behind snowbanks or in the low groves of cedar and birch.

One night, the mail never arrived. Later, they found the sled—upturned and splintered. The dogs lay silent. The man's body was never recovered. Only blood in the snow.

The killer was never caught.

Some believe he still walks the woods. But others say the mailman returns, searching the route with a lantern's glow, drawn back to the place where his journey ended too soon.

The Light Still Moves

Today, travelers still pull over on Robbins Pond Road, where the old trail meets modern asphalt. They kill their lights and wait. The forest does not speak. The wind does not blow.

And then—the glow.

Some say it blinks like a swinging lantern. Others swear it trails after cars, keeping pace just behind the taillights.

A few never see it at all.

But those who do… never forget.

If you find yourself near Dog Meadow, past sundown, and the forest seems to be watching—stop.

If the light comes, do not follow it.

Some roads were never meant to be traveled twice.

Michigan: The Drowned Girl—Beckoning Minnie

A Town Fed by Timber and Ghosts

In the 1800s, the town of Forester, Michigan, thrived where the timber met the lake. Lumber crews stalked the forests, and steamships lined up along Lake Huron's shoreline, their hulls packed with pine. The scent of sawdust clung to the wind, and the air was always thick with work. But under that hum of commerce, something else stirred. Something older. Something colder.

When the lake called, it never gave back what it took.

The Girl Who Loved a Ghost

In May of 1861, Minnie Quay was born into this churning place of wood, water, and iron. After turning fourteen, she had fallen deeply and desperately in love—with a nameless sailor whose ship often docked at the Forester port.

He was older. Untethered.

She was smitten. Her parents were furious.

Her mother, Mary Ann Quay, was said to have screamed in a rage: "I would rather see Minnie dead than with that sailor!"

The lake, they said, hears all things.

And it remembers curses better than most.

The Storm That Broke Her

In the spring of 1876, the sailor's ship never returned.

A storm had engulfed Lake Huron—the sails were torn like the fragile wings of a butterfly ripped from its body by a tornado, and the hull splintered easily like frail old bones beaten with a bat, and then dragged beneath gray waves.

When the news reached Minnie, something inside her split. She became silent. Detached. Eyes too wide, voice too calm. She no longer spoke of the future. She watched the shoreline. And then, one April morning, while left alone to care for her little brother, Minnie walked to Smith's dock. The lake was still that day.

But she was not. Without a cry, without even removing her shoes, she threw herself into the freezing black water.

By the time anyone found her, she had already sunk.

And she never stopped sinking.

The Girl Who Beckons the Living

They buried Minnie on a bluff overlooking the lake. Her grave still stands—weathered and watched. But it wasn't long before something began to stir again.

At first, just whispers among the fishermen—an oddly pale girl walking the dock in the dead of night, the hem of her dress soaked, her hair clinging to her neck.

Then came the stories from travelers, who swore they saw her pacing the sand, lips moving soundlessly, always staring out across the water.

But it got worse.

Much worse. Young women began to report the same thing: A girl in white. Waving. Smiling faintly. *Motioning for them to come closer to the lake.* Urging them with eyes that held no light, only sorrow.

Some resisted. Not all did.

The Grave That Hungers

To this day, visitors still find their way to Minnie Quay's grave, leaving behind pennies, flowers, and locks of hair—small offerings meant to appease her spirit.

They whisper apologies.

They beg for safe passage home.

Because it is said that if you don't pay her respect, she might follow you. She might slip into your dreams, her soaked fingers tapping at your window.

She might whisper your name as you stare into your own mirror.

And if you find yourself near the dock, the bluff, and the bone-deep silence of Lake Huron's shallows…You might hear a splash.

You might see her waving.

You might start walking, unaware your body has begun to move toward the water.

And by the time you realize what's happening—you're already waist-deep.

And she is already holding your hand, tugging you in with her.

Minnesota: Bobbing Lantern of Arcola High Bridge

Steel Above, Shadows Below

Stretching like a skeletal arm across the St. Croix River, the Arcola High Bridge cuts through the sky—a rusted monument to a war long past. Beneath it, the waters churn cold and black. Along the Arcola Bluffs Day Use Area trails, visitors hike beneath the towering trestle, where the wind sings frantically like it remembers something horrible happened there. However, it simply cannot recall what it is.

But if you stay too long after dusk, you might see it. A blue light. Flickering. Bobbing. Swaying like it's being carried by someone who shouldn't be walking at all.

The Watchman's Last Night

During the panic of World War I, the bridge served as a vital artery—hauling crates of ammunition from the Twin Cities Army Ammunition Plant, the cargo hurtling eastward across the St. Croix toward unknown battlefields. To protect this precious cargo from sabotage or enemy hands, a night watchman was stationed at the bridge. He was never named in the papers. Just another uniform. Another body guarding the war machine.

One storm-soaked night, thunder roared like gunfire as the watchman made his rounds. Lantern in hand, slick with rain, he began his walk across the bridge.

And then—the train came.

No one knows whether they mistimed the schedule or the storm masked the sound. But what they found the next morning was not a body. *They found pieces.*

His coat was shredded and twisted in the rail ties. A lantern was bent into a crescent shape with a blood-soaked glove curled into a fist. His head was never found.

The Lantern That Won't Go Out

That should've been the end. But it wasn't.

Now, on certain nights, the lantern returns. It floats above the rails, its light casting a sickly blue pallor, like a wound that won't heal. Behind it, a shadow strolls—a man who doesn't walk so much as jerk forward, limbs unnatural, boots dragging, head tilted like it's trying to rest on a neck that no longer supports it.

Some say he's looking for his missing parts.

Others say he doesn't know he's dead.

But all agree: he's still watching the bridge. Still guarding the path.

He was still waiting for a train that had already taken him.

He Comes Closer Than You Think

Visitors near the bridge have reported more than light. Some have heard the screech of metal on metal, with no train in sight. Others say their phones fail. Cameras go black. The air goes suddenly icy—and the smell of wet iron and burned oil fills their lungs.

One hiker swore he saw the watchman up close. Said the man had no lower jaw, just a dark dripping cavity and a twisting tongue trying to speak.

"I think he tried to warn me," he said. "But all I could hear was… the sound of a train coming."

If you walk the Arcola Bluffs trail after dark and see a light on the tracks—don't follow it.

If you hear footsteps behind you, don't stop. Because the watchman isn't just looking after the bridge.

He's looking for someone to take his place.

Mississippi: Old Man Stuckey's Remains

Old, winding roads slice through the dense Mississippi woodland, twisting from faded asphalt to gravel until the tires finally crunch into blood-red dirt. These roads—forgotten by most but not by the dead—lead the daring to a place the locals whisper about: Stuckey's Bridge, a rusting steel truss and rot that claws across the Chunky River, about twelve miles outside Meridian.

They say the bridge groans when no one is walking it.

They say something still walks it anyway.

The Man Who Slept Beside Corpses

The story begins with Old Man Stuckey, a name that still makes dogs howl low when it's whispered near the river. According to legend, he was a one-time accomplice of the Dalton Gang, the infamous outlaws who painted their names across banks and trains with blood and gunpowder between 1890 and 1892.

Stuckey wasn't famous like the Dalton brothers. He didn't ride into town firing pistols. But he could easily have passed as their kin with all the evil within him.

He waited. He watched. And then he killed.

They say he ran a roadside inn not far from the bridge. A quiet, creaking house near the river's bend. Travelers came and went—until they *didn't*. Stuckey would feed them, joke with them, wait until they slept, and then drag them—thrashing and half-strangled—down to the riverbank. There, he split them open like filleting a fish. He buried their remains deep beneath the mud or else let the current take them. Twenty bodies. Maybe more.

He slit throats with the same blade he used to cut bread. He smiled while he did it.

The Hanging

Finally, the law caught up to him. Stuckey was seized and dragged to the bridge that had stood silently through his crimes. They tied the noose. They let him look down into the river that had hidden his sins. And then they dropped him. When his body swung to stillness, the air grew cold. And when they cut him down, his corpse hit the water with a wet slap so loud it echoed into the woods like a gunshot. That's when the absolute terror began.

The Lantern That Still Burns

But Stuckey didn't sink forever.

Not completely.

Now, on certain nights—when the mist hangs low and the river moans through the rocks—a pale lantern appears beneath the bridge. It sways slowly along the shoreline, bobbing up and down like it's being carried by a man whose legs no longer move right. His back hunched, his jaw slack from the noose that stretched it.

His eyes are open.

Wide.

Bulging.

Unblinking.

Some have seen him up close—wading just beneath the water's surface, his skeletal hand outstretched as if still trying to drag something—or someone—back with him.

Others hear only the splash.

That final sound.

Over and over again.

Mississippi: The Angel That Watches the Dead... and the Living

The Inferno on Main and Union

In the heart of Natchez, Mississippi, where the heat clings heavy and the river drags its weight in silence, there once stood a tidy brick building on the corner of Main and Union—the Natchez Drug Company, owned by the well-regarded John H. Chambliss. Four floors tall, it loomed quietly over the city. But beneath its polished counters and glass jars, a monster had been installed—a gas-fired stove, newly fitted in the laboratory upstairs.

Pipes snaked through the walls like veins. They were meant to bring warmth. Instead, they would deliver death. Among those who helped install the piping was Sam Burns, who was just 21 years old. A plumber. A volunteer fireman. A young man too brave to be careful.

March 14, 1908 – The Smell of Doom

On a deceptively bright spring morning, workers inside the building noted something wrong—a heavy smell of gas, thick and unnatural, slithering up from the shadows. It clung to their clothes. It coated their throats. But by early afternoon, they'd grown used to it.

Sam Burns arrived just after noon. He lit a small candle, its innocent flicker dancing in his steady hand. Back then, it was common. Accepted. Deadly.

He began on the fourth floor. Then he moved to the basement. And at 2:45 p.m., time stopped.

With a sound like the sky being torn open, the Natchez Drug Company detonated. Flames and debris exploded outward, ripping bodies apart mid-breath. The brick rained down like shrapnel. Glass melted. Flesh turned to smoke. Pieces of women, men, and children were hurled through the air, organs fused to walls, bones splintered, hearts split open, and left steaming in the street.

Children in the Ashes

Eleven people died that day. Five were children—young employees, ages 12 to 21, caught in the inferno with no warning, chance, or way out. Their screams were said to echo for hours afterward—whether in the rubble or in the minds of those who survived, no one could be sure.

Workers sifted through what was left when the fires died and the soot settled. They didn't find bodies. They found limbs. A scorched scalp. Charred vertebrae stacked like blackened coins. A pile of hands, some still clenched—some open, as if pleading. Even pedestrians walking outside the building—people simply passing by—were torn to pieces.

The Angel That Mourns… and Moves

The owner, John H. Chambliss, never recovered from what happened in his building. In an act of mourning—or maybe guilt—he commissioned a towering marble angel to watch over the graves of the five young victims buried at Natchez City Cemetery.

She stands with wings folded, eyes downcast, one hand reaching as if still trying to catch the falling. The angel was meant to honor the dead. But she doesn't rest.

People who drive Cemetery Road at night, headlights cutting through the stillness, say the same thing:

"She turns."

Her face, fixed in stone, seems to follow. Her gaze shifts. Her sorrow becomes suspicion. Her hand seems to point not toward heaven but toward the street—toward the living. Some say she only turns to those who don't know the story.

Others say she watches everyone.

Waiting. Warning. Weeping.

If you drive past the Natchez City Cemetery after dark, keep your eyes ahead. Because if you meet her gaze in your rearview mirror, she may follow you home. She knows who forgot the fire. She knows who turned away.

Missouri: The Haunting of Bloody Hill

A Field Drenched in Blood

On August 10, 1861, the wilderness near Wilson's Creek, Missouri, erupted into chaos. Union and Confederate forces clashed in the humid morning air—bayonets glinting, smoke thick as fog, and screams rising like hymns from Hell. The battle lasted hours. The ground ran wet with so much blood shed from men and boys, it was called Bloody Hill. When the smoke cleared, more than 2,500 men lay dead, dying, or mutilated.

Their bodies, tangled in heaps, limbs blown apart by cannon fire or split by musket balls, fed the red clay. The Union lost Brigadier General Nathaniel Lyon, the first Union general to be killed in the Civil War. His shattered body was left slumped in the dirt, riddled with bullets.

The Confederates claimed the field.

But the field—it claimed them all.

Where the Dead Refuse to Sleep

Today, the battlefield is calm.

Too calm.

Trees have grown where men fell. The tall grass shivers in the wind. But those who wander the grounds after dark say the calm is a veil.

Visitors report hearing the crack of rifles and the thunder of an invisible cannon.

Sometimes, the air stinks of gunpowder and rotting flesh.

Others have listened to the screams of horses and the gurgling gasps of men who no longer breathe.

And then there are the figures. Shadowy soldiers drift through the woods, half-formed, some missing arms or legs, others with faces half blown away—their jaws swinging loose, their eyes empty sockets.

One man was seen crawling, his spine exposed, dragging himself through the dirt as if still trying to reach his regiment.

One hiker saw a line of Confederates standing silently beneath the trees—motionless, faceless, their coats bloodstained and eyes glowing like dying embers.

When he blinked, they were gone.

But the air hadn't cooled.

It had grown colder.

The Battle Still Rages

What happened at Wilson's Creek was not confined to the history books. The land remembers. The dead were buried in haste, often in shallow trenches or burned in heaps. Some were never found at all—swallowed by the earth, their bones tangled in roots, their agony soaked into the soil.

And so, they rise.

Not to fight for the Union.

Not for the Confederacy.

But for vengeance, for peace, for release.

Or maybe they don't rise at all.

Maybe they never fell.

Maybe the battle never ended.

If you walk Wilson's Creek at night, listen.

Every footstep echoes. Every whisper might be a scream. And when the wind carries the stench of smoke and blood, don't look back.

Because something still walks there.

Something without a face. Without a cause.

Only the memory of savagery.

Montana: Sister Irene Will Not Rest in Virginia City

Gold and Graves in Alder Gulch

In 1863 men clawed through the soil of Alder Gulch, unearthing not just gold, but the bones of a boomtown. Virginia City, Montana, rose with violent speed, built atop the fever of fortune. By 1865, more than 5,000 souls had poured in—miners, gamblers, drifters, and the damned. But gold is never eternal. When the veins ran dry, the people bled away leaving behind empty streets, rotting beams, and stories whispered in the wind.

Yet not everyone left. Some still remain.

The Bonanza Inn and the Rooms That Remember

At the height of its chaos, the Bonanza Inn became a place not of rest, but of ruin. Repurposed as a hospital in the 1870s, it was managed by the Sisters of Charity, women of God cloaked in black, tending to the broken, the diseased, and the dying. Among them was Sister Irene—known for her stillness, her silence, and her gaze that never blinked when faced with death.

She lived long enough to see the gold fade, the walls crumble, and the town fall quiet. When she finally died at age 87, they buried her near the place where she had watched so many others pass.

But she didn't stay in the ground.

The Return of the Black Robe

Today, Virginia City is preserved in time, a historical husk. Visitors tour its buildings, snapping photos and rattling through gift shops. But some speak of a presence—not a relic of the past, but a shadow of it.

Inside the former hospital, things are not right. Doorknobs twist slowly in the silence. Footsteps tap through hallways where no shoes walk. And sometimes, from the corner of your eye, you might see her:

A tall woman in a black robe, her face hidden beneath a heavy veil, glides from room to room as though she still carries her final patient—or worse, searches for the next. Her footsteps are slow. Measured. Solemn. Yet for reasons lost to time, she did not find rest in the grave.

Because she can't stop caring. It is her duty. Even in death.

She Still Walks

They say Sister Irene still strolls around the hospital, searching for someone to tend to—whether they are sick or not.

And she will not stop until she finds someone.

Anyone.

Perhaps that's why, when the hallway grows quiet and the doorknob begins to turn, it's already too late.

She's chosen you.

Nebraska: Don't Look Too Long in the Platte River

The Witch's Curse

Just south of Grand Island, Nebraska, a narrow, one-lane bridge stretches across the Platte River like a wound pulled taut. Long ago, a woman who practiced witchcraft made her home at one end.

She cursed those who crossed, and though her body is long gone, her hatred lingers—etched into the wood, buried in the current. You can hear her humming beneath the rusted bolts. *Hmmmm. Hmmmm.*

They say if an odd-numbered group stands on the bridge on an odd-numbered night and peers into the water, they'll see something unnatural:

Themselves—hanging. *Hmmmm. Hmmmm.*

Slack-jawed. Lifeless. Dangling just beneath the surface. *Hmmmm. Hmmmm.*

But if they look too long, the witch comes for them—rising from the depths in silence, her fingers cold and clawed—humming, humming, humming that damnable noise that makes them dizzy—to pull them down forever.

Things That Go Bump in the Night

Nebraska: The Blood that Soaked Seven Sisters Road

A House of Pain, Just Beyond the Trees

In the spring of 1886, deep in the country near what is now known as Seven Sisters Road, a farmhouse stood as a prison for two children. From the outside, the land was quiet—nothing but dirt, dust, and the chirping of birds. But inside that house, something monstrous lived. Lee Shellenberger was a brute cloaked in the disguise of a farmer. He lived there with his second wife, Marinda, and his two children—Joe, aged fourteen, and Maggie, ten.

He ruled the house with a whip, its lash more familiar to his daughter than a father's gentle hand.

Maggie was beaten often, and Lee made no secret of his hatred for her. Neighbors would later say he enjoyed hurting her—taking pride in the way her small body flinched when he reached for the strap. She tried to run away. Many times. Once to a neighbor. Another time, toward Missouri, to her grandparents. But every time, he dragged her back.

And each time, he punished her harder.

One day, he promised: "If you ever run again, I'll cut your throat from ear to ear."

He meant it.

April 30, 1886 – The Slaughter in the Cellar

They found Maggie's body the day before her 11th birthday in a dark cellar beneath the house. Her throat had indeed been cut—not once, but five times—deep gashes that nearly severed her head. She lay slumped across a dry goods bin, blood-soaked and broken. Blood filled the container and splashed the walls three feet away as if the room itself had tried to scream.

The blade: a wooden-handled butcher knife.

The killer: her father—or perhaps, both him and Marinda. A doctor testified later that no human could have cut their own throat like that, not with such brutality, not so many times. Yet Lee claimed she'd done it herself. The court didn't believe him. Neither did the townspeople. Especially when it came to light that Maggie was the heir to valuable property—land that would go to her father if she died.

The Mob, the Rope, and the Curse

The town erupted in fury. A mob of masked men, many believed to be local farmers, stormed the jail. They broke into the sheriff's office above the cells, dragged Lee Shellenberger out by the neck, and hanged him from a tree right outside the courthouse.

No last words.

No prayer.

Just the sound of a body swinging in the wind.

And Marinda, his wife? She faded from public record, her fate uncertain—perhaps escaping the rope, but never the curse.

Seven Sisters Road—Where the Dead Still Speak

Today, the winding stretch known as Seven Sisters Road—labeled Road L on the maps—cuts through that same land. It's quiet, but only during the day. At night, the trees tremble. People say you can hear Maggie's screams in the woods if you roll down your windows. If you stop on the bridge, your car might stall, your lights might die, and a voice might whisper your name in that black silence.

Sometimes, people see two glowing red eyes in the treetops.

Not animal. Not human.

Something twisted. Watching.

They say it's Lee Shellenberger, risen from the pit, looking for vengeance—not just on the town that hanged him, but on anyone who dares cross the road he once ruled with blood.

And sometimes, when the wind is just right, you may see a little girl in white standing near the ditch, her hand raised—not waving, but warning.

Don't go further.

Don't let him find you.

Because maybe Maggie's spirit knows something we don't.

Maybe she knows her father escaped Hell.

And maybe she's trying to stop you before he drags you back with him.

Nevada: The Mysterious Woman in White of Virginia City

She floats Through the Streets

A mysterious woman cloaked in a tattered white gown drifts through the streets of Virginia City, Nevada, her form barely touching the earth. Wherever she passes, the air turns cold—as if the town itself holds its breath.

Whispers trail behind her, disembodied and unintelligible, and some swear they hear weeping just beneath the wind. However, no source can ever be found.

She is Mysterious

No one knows her name. No one remembers her face. But they say she came from the city's violent mining boom, a time when the streets ran thick with greed, blood, and unmarked graves.

Now she wanders the ruins of that history, still searching for something lost—or someone who wronged her.

And when the night is quiet enough, she weeps for all of them.

New Hampshire: The Staircase to Nowhere in the Woods

What's Hidden in the Forest

Deep in the shadowed forests of West Chesterfield, New Hampshire, a ruin sleeps beneath moss and memory. The trees here lean in as if whispering about the woman who once built a castle among them. She was known as Madame Sherri, though her real name was Antoinette DeLilas—a Paris-born costume designer and former showgirl who drifted from the theaters of New York to the calm of rural New England in the late 1920s.

But Madame Sherri didn't come to disappear quietly.

She came to build a kingdom of smoke, silk, and scandal away from prying eyes.

The Castle in the Woods

They called it a castle, though it was more like a bizarre fever dream—half-French chalet, half-Roman ruin, with towering stone walls, a vaulted barroom where trees pierced the ceiling, and a grand curving staircase that led into the forest like it belonged in an opera set.

In the cellar: an intimate bistro lit by wine-glass chandeliers. In the bedrooms above: mystery, whispers, and perhaps things more sinister.

Madame Sherri arrived at the building site dressed in velvet, lace, or nothing appropriate at all. Some said she wore silk robes that dragged across the floor; others swore she draped herself in fox fur and pearls in the pouring rain. She gave parties beneath the trees, where the music swelled, and strangers danced barefoot on the moss, vanishing before dawn.

The Fire That Took Everything

By the late 1950s, the forest had begun to reclaim her paradise. The castle crumbled. Moss bloomed over banisters. The laughter faded.

Then, on October 20, 1962, it burned. The cause? Unknown. Some say she lit the fire herself. Others believe the woods were tired of her decadence, and something darker consumed it from within. All that remains now is the staircase, rising from the earth like a stone ribcage, leading nowhere.

Or perhaps—somewhere we shouldn't follow.

But She Never Left

To this day, hikers report strange things near the ruins.

A cold spot at the base of the stairs.

Laughter drifts through the trees when no one is there.

The faint clinking of champagne glasses.

Some have seen her—a veiled figure in black, standing at the top of the broken staircase, watching.

Waiting.

"Come," she seems to say. "The party isn't over."

And perhaps, for Madame Sherri, it never will be.

New Hampshire: The Pale Sentinel of White Island

Where treasure sleeps beneath stone and sorrow, and something dead still waits.

Edward Teach—Blackbeard—was no ordinary pirate. He was a monster draped in man's flesh, feared from the blood-soaked coasts of the Carolinas to the icy shores of New England. With a beard tangled in ribbons and fire and pistols strapped across his chest like ribs, he carved terror into the hearts of all who crossed him.

But even monsters harbor secrets.

He hid more than gold among the wind-ravaged Isles of Shoals, tucked between Maine and New Hampshire. On White Island, he kept a woman.

What the Pirate Secreted

She was said to be a Scottish girl, stolen from her village and taken across the sea by force.

But the sea changed her.

Or perhaps he did.

Whatever the reason, she came to love him. Or perhaps it was fear twisted into something that looked like love.

A Promise Bound in Blood

One fog-thick dawn, a panicked sailor rushed up the rocks to warn Blackbeard—a ship approached. The sea churned with war. Before he left, the pirate flung his white cloak around the girl's shoulders.

"Guard the treasure with your life," he told her, placing the final weight of his sin on her frail shoulders.

Then he vanished into the storm.

Cannons thundered. The sea exploded with fire. When the smoke cleared, both ships were gone, shattered to bone and iron.

Survivors reached land—but the winter devoured them all.

She alone remained, starving, cradling gold that could not feed her.

Still wearing that cursed white cloak, her ribs pressing through skin, she perished on the rocks, staring forever toward the water where his ship vanished.

The Lady in the Cloak Still Waits

They say she's still there.

On stormy nights, her specter rises from the cliffs, cloaked in salt-stained white, her hair matted with seaweed, her mouth a black slit of hunger, her voice a hollow whisper on the wind:

"He will come for me."

Some fishermen have glimpsed her pale figure staring from the rocks, eyes like hollow shells, her cloak flapping as if caught in a wind that doesn't blow.

Those who dare anchor too close speak of terrible dreams—of gold coins choking their throats, of a dead woman clawing her way into their boats, whispering her pirate's name.

And on the coldest nights, the sea still booms with phantom cannon fire while a white shape stands sentinel on White Island, guarding treasure no one dares claim.

New Jersey: The Dead Boy Beneath the Bridge on Clinton Road

Clinton Road remembers. Especially the drowned.

A bridge crosses Mossman Brook, just beyond the sickening bend called Dead Man's Curve on Clinton Road in West Milford, New Jersey. It's older than most remember, and the pavement groans when you cross it as if burdened by something buried below. They say a little boy died here, his small body swept beneath the current, his lungs filled with black water. Some say he slipped while playing. Others whisper he was pushed.

However, he died, and he never left.

He Hates to Be Forgotten

At night, something stirs if you stop on the bridge and drop a coin into the brook. You might hear a splash… then nothing.

Until the coin comes flicking back out of the darkness, wet, cold, and impossible.

Sometimes, it hits the road. Sometimes it hits you. Locals swear they've seen tiny wet footprints on the asphalt, leading from the water to nowhere. And if you stay too long—if you listen too closely—you'll hear something worse. Crying.

Or worse still: Giggling.

Don't Look Over the Edge

Some have looked over the rail to see a pale hand just under the surface, grasping at the air, waiting.

One woman said she saw a face below the water—bloated, greenish-white, the mouth wide open, lips curled back from rotting baby teeth.

Another man claimed something grabbed his wrist, trying to drag him in. He never drives Clinton Road anymore.

He's Still Down There

They say if you drop your coin in and don't wait for it to return, you've taken something from him. And he'll follow you. Some say that's why the curve is called Dead Man's Curve—not because of the road's shape, but because those who see the boy's face…don't always make it home.

New Mexico: Mysterious Cemetery Lights in Dawson

The Hell Beneath Dawson

Once a flourishing coal town nestled in the rugged folds of northeastern New Mexico, Dawson rose quickly from dust and ambition in 1901. Built near the Vermejo River, it boasted all the modern amenities a miner's family could dream of—churches, a hospital, a school, and even a golf course. Dawson was a company town, yes—but it was proud, bustling, and full of life.

Until it wasn't.

The Hell Below—The First Collapse

On a bitter October morning in 1913, the earth split open. An explosion deep within the Stag Canyon Mine No. 2 shook the entire valley. The blast killed 263 men—fathers, sons, brothers. The initial shockwave turned tunnels into tombs. Fire and black smoke spewed from the mouth of the mine. Most of the dead were entombed where they stood, buried alive in darkness, their skin seared by coal dust and fire, lungs scorched from the inside. A rescue team clawed into the pit with shovels and bleeding hands, only to find the dead locked in poses of terror—some curled in prayer, others with broken fingernails scraping at the walls.

Their charred remains were hauled out and laid beneath the same sun that had risen on them hours before, the air now thick with ash and grief. Families watched silently as wagon after wagon rolled by, covered in sheets, leaking blood.

The Second Death

Ten years later, it happened again. March 1923. Stag Canyon Mine No. 1. Another explosion. Another 123 men were erased. Their deaths were quieter but no less cruel—some smothered by gas before they could scream, others crushed by the collapsing vein of coal that had fed the town. After that, Dawson began to rot.

The Bones of the Town

The mines closed. The buildings decayed. The wind reclaimed the streets, the trees tore through roofs, and the silence moved in like a fog. Today, Dawson is barely a ghost. But its cemetery remains. And it whispers.

Row after row of white iron crosses—over 350—jut from the dirt like skeletal teeth. Each one marks the body of a man who went into the earth and never truly came back.

Their names fade in rust, but the ground remembers.

Visitors speak of glowing helmet lights bobbing in the darkness, weaving among the graves. These lights never break the silence; they only hover, blink, and vanish.

Some say they're the spirits of men still trying to find their way home.

Others tell of whispers in languages long gone—Italian, Greek, Polish—calling out from beneath the dry, cracked soil.

There are stories of footsteps echoing down the trail when no one walks it, of a cold coal dust smell that settles on the tongue and won't go away.

And some see more.

They see faces.

Twisted, sooty, eyeless. Pressed up from beneath the ground. Or watching from the tree line. Their mouths open, not in warning—but in agony.

The mine is closed, yes.

But something beneath Dawson still breathes.

Still waits.

Still burns.

Still keeps the dead in her arms, never letting them leave.

Still, they try.

Again and again and again.

New York: The Weeping Widow of Amsterdam

There is a Lonely Road

There is a lonely stretch of road in Amsterdam, New York, where the trees lean in, and the air thickens with sorrow. Locals call it Widow Susan Road. Few linger here after dusk. And those who do often return... changed. It is said that the road earned its name not from folklore but from a real woman—Susan Thomas DeGraff, widowed in 1848 when her husband, Hermanus DeGraff, died at just 43.

Hermanus was believed to have been buried in the DeGraff family cemetery, tucked into the wilderness near the corner of what is now East Main Street and the road that would bear the widow's name.

The graveyard has long since fallen to ruin, its stones broken, names erased by time.

After Hermanus's death, Susan lived on for over four decades.

The townsfolk, half with pity, half with disdain, came to call her Widow Susan.

She died at the age of 72 in 1892, her body laid to rest not beside her husband but alone—in Green Hill Cemetery, far from the DeGraff family plot, which by then had become overgrown and forgotten.

And that is why she cannot rest.

Searching the Wrong Graves

It began with soft sobbing. Whispered weeping carried by the wind.

Then came the sightings. A pale figure dressed in a long, tattered white gown was seen wandering the old DeGraff Cemetery—her back hunched, her hands outstretched, dragging through grass and soil as if to uncover someone lost beneath.

Witnesses say her face is obscured, veiled in darkness, but the sound of her grief can chill the marrow.

Others have claimed to see her outside Saint Casimir Cemetery or Saint Nicholas Cemetery as if she no longer remembers where he was buried or why they were separated.

The most disturbing reports come from those who have watched her cry before a headstone, only for her to lift her face, mouth agape in silent horror, as if something is terribly wrong—as if what lies beneath the soil is not her husband at all.

A Warning in the Fog

Drivers along Widow Susan Road sometimes find their headlights flicker as a sudden mist coils across the road.

Some say a woman in white crosses in front of them, pausing just long enough to be seen before she vanishes into the trees.

If you see her, you must not stop. You must not speak to her.

She is still searching.

And she is no longer sure who she's searching for.

It just might be you she follows.

Or worse yet, takes to the grave with her.

New York: The Restless Beneath: Washington Square Park

They Lay Below

Washington Square Park—green, bustling, lively—is a mask. Beneath its cobblestone veins and curated trees lies a nightmare buried deep, clawing for remembrance. Long before jazz musicians and chess players claimed the corners, this land was something else before the arch threw its triumphant shadow onto the square.

Something darker.

In the 17th century, it belonged to the Lenape, a Native people who called the land Sapokanican. Then came the Dutch, calling it New Amsterdam.

And as cities grow, so do the dead.

The Potter's Field

From 1797 to 1825, during New York's grisliest epidemics, the land was turned into a potter's field—a mass graveyard for the nameless and unwanted.

Victims of yellow fever were carted in by the hundreds, their bodies heaped into trenches by the weak light of lanterns.

The sick were feared and discarded.

More than 20,000 corpses were dumped and layered beneath the soil—limbs tangled, mouths agape, eyes frozen in the agony of fevered death. The reek of decay, rotting corpses, and tang of sickness fouled the air. No handkerchief or palm could conceal the horrible stench that swept from the ground, winding through the streets and lingering for blocks.

The city closed the field, but not the wound.

In 1825, they simply paved over the dead. Grass grew. Children played. But the screams and whispers remained.

The ground had been fed, and it had not forgotten.

The Hanging Tree

In 1819, under the bent arms of what is now known as the Hangman's Elm, the state hanged 19-year-old Rose Butler. She had been convicted of setting a fire in the home where she was enslaved.

Her death was a spectacle—hundreds watched her dangle, gasping her last breath in the pestilent air of a death-soaked field. Hers was one of the final public executions in the city, but not the last soul to cry out here.

Her body vanished into the trenches. But not for long.

Ghosts Who Walk in Silence

By the mid-19th century, the park was redesigned—new trees planted, new monuments built, and a great white arch raised like a bone out of the past. But the dead stirred beneath, unsettled by the weight of celebration.

They do not rest.

Witnesses speak of cold spots on summer days.

Spectral figures in colonial rags flicker into view, mouths moving in silent gasps before vanishing behind trees. Laughter that trails off mid-breath.

Pale women in graveclothes pacing the cobblestones in the hours just before dawn.

A man, eyes wide with terror, seen only in reflection, mouthing something soundless beneath the arch.

There are reports—quiet, often whispered—of unnatural movement in the trees. Particularly the Elm. The branches shift and stretch when the wind is still. Some say it is just the breeze.

Others say it's the rope. Still hanging.

And sometimes, very late, the ground exhales. Cold breath from below.

The weight of a thousand hands pressing upward from forgotten soil.

North Carolina: The Tar River Banshee

The Tar River, winding like a dark ribbon through northeastern North Carolina, has always carried more than just water. Stretching over 200 miles through dense woods, silent hollows, and mist-choked lowlands, its murky depths were once a lifeline for the colonies—a passageway for tar, pitch, and turpentine that fueled the shipbuilding industry.

But history stains its banks, and something unearthly remains.

He was a Patriot

In the final bitter years of the Revolutionary War, David Warner, an English-born settler and miller, found himself torn between blood and conviction. Though a subject of the Crown, he aligned himself with the American cause, quietly supplying Patriot troops with flour and provisions from his riverside mill.

It was a risky defiance—and it did not go unnoticed.

But the British Found Out Whose Side He was On

On a blistering hot August afternoon in 1781, five British scouts rode into the woods near the Tar River. They found Warner alone at his mill, grinding grain with the steady rhythm of one who knew he was being watched—and did not care.

They bound him at the edge of the river.

But before the final act, Warner reportedly stared into the eyes of his executioners and issued a chilling warning:

"If you kill me, a banshee will rise from this river and drag your souls screaming to Hell."

The Drowned Him, Laughing

They drowned him with mocking laughter where the waters turn deepest, lashing a millstone to his body and watching him vanish without a bubble.

The Banshee Wailed

That night, the wailing began. It was not the wind.

Witnesses heard a piercing, unnatural scream rise from the banks—a sound so mournful and shrill it shattered the air like glass.

The men who killed Warner were all found days later, one by one, their faces contorted in utter terror, blood crusted in their ears. It was as if something had screamed so loudly it burst their minds from within.

The Banshee, locals say, never returned to the depths.

She is still there.

She is seen drifting barefoot along the riverbank, her soaked black gown clinging to her body, her long, tangled hair veiling a face that shifts between sorrow and rage. Her eyes reflect no light. She opens her mouth, and though no breath escapes, a sound erupts that freezes blood and crushes hearts.

They say She Searches for Others.

On humid August nights, when the river sweats and the trees press close with their suffocating silence, you may hear her cry—high, jagged, unending.

Sometimes, she is seen perched on a rock in the middle of the river, keening like a broken mother.

Sometimes, she stands beside the water, staring across it as if waiting for someone… or something… to return. Some believe it's Warner.

Others think she guards the river so no other soul may pass without judgment.

Whatever the truth, if you ever find yourself on the banks of the Tar after dark and the air begins to hum with silence—run. Don't listen. Don't look.

Because if she sees you… she is still seeking out those the miller cursed.

And she won't stop until he returns.

North Carolina: Lost Cove—Where Ghosts Linger

A Refuge from War's Reach

In the twilight of the Civil War, Morgan Bailey led his family into the mountains. He wasn't searching for fortune. He was searching for quiet.

He found it in a lonely hollow near the North Carolina–Tennessee borderland so remote it seemed untouched by the bloodshed sweeping the South. There, he carved a life from rock and root in the cradle of Pisgah National Forest.

Others followed The Tiptons. The Millers. Men and women with names now nearly erased who built a town they hoped would remain unseen.

They called it Lost Cove.

A Town Between States

From the start, Lost Cove was a town without clear borders—perched where one state faded into another, forgotten by both. This made it difficult to govern.

And easy to disappear into.

The families farmed. Grew tomatoes, apples, potatoes. Logged the forest's tall timber. They raised livestock and children. They endured. But when the economy soured, and survival grew steep, many turned to what the land would let them make in secret: moonshine.

The Whispering Stills

In the deep woods, hidden stills bubbled and steamed beneath pine boughs. Moonshine wasn't just a tradition—it was currency. A way to endure harsh winters and feed large families.

Federal agents found it difficult to intervene with no clear law enforcement jurisdiction. Lost Cove was a gray area. A blind spot. A ghost on a map that never wanted visitors.

Some say strange things happened near the still sites—echoes where there should be silence. Steam that drifted the wrong way.

A still man once claimed he heard a voice in the trees repeating back everything he said, one word behind.

He dismantled his still the next day.

The Quiet Decline

By the mid-20th century, Lost Cove was fading. You couldn't drive in. Supplies had to be carried by foot or rail.

The railroad stopped running. The schoolhouse fell quiet. Families left one by one, carried out by time and hardship. There were no fires. No grand calamity. Just the slow, quiet surrender of wood to moss and roofs to rain.

The forest did not rush.

It waited.

The Last to Leave

On January 1, 1958, Velmer Bailey and his family packed what they could carry and walked away from Lost Cove. They were the last.

What they left behind crumbled slowly. Homes fell in. Porches rotted. Trees pushed up through kitchen floors.

The bones of the town sank into the earth.

People say Velmer never spoke much about those final months. But once, when asked why they didn't stay, he said: "It didn't want us there anymore."

What Remains

Hikers who find their way to the old site say it feels wrong. Not violent. Just heavy. Still.

You can still find remnants if you know where to look. A rusted bedframe under a collapsed roof. A school bell half-buried in vines. The caved-in chimney of the Bailey home. And sometimes, apple trees bloom at the forest's edge, far from where orchards once stood.

But no one picks the fruit. And no one stays the night.

Shhh. Listen. The Old Ghosts are Still There

Those who stray too far off the trail say the woods begin to listen.

Branches creak in still air.

Shadows shift just a little too slowly.

A few claim they've heard a faint knock—not near, but beneath them. Like something tapping on a door long gone. Voices of those who once lived there. Died there. Still tarry long after they were buried underground.

If you find yourself in Lost Cove, walk lightly.

Some say Lost Cove died when its families left.

But others say it went quiet.

And in the deep hush between the trees, it's still listening.

Still watching.

Waiting for someone to call it home again.

North Dakota: Riverside Cemetery—Knock-Knock Ghost

The Knock-Knock That Comes Back

Founded in the 1870s, Riverside Cemetery sprawls across the edge of Fargo like a city of the dead—its gates flanked by iron, its paths shadowed by old trees that don't sway, even when the wind howls.

It is the largest burial ground in the Fargo-Moorhead area. And perhaps the loudest.

A mausoleum with no name on the door stands among its worn headstones and crumbling monuments. Just a faded plaque, half-pried loose by time and trembling hands. Locals say if you knock-knock on it, it knock-knocks back. Not an echo. Not a vibration.

A reply. One solid, deliberate knock. Sometimes two. And sometimes, if you wait too long, a third knock will come—from behind you. *Knock-knock-knock*

The Voice Inside the Vault

Some claim they've heard a voice—dry, crumbling—calling out from within the sealed stone.

It doesn't call for help. *It calls your name.*

One boy, dared by friends, placed his ear to the door and swore he heard someone whisper, "Where have you been?" He refused to return to the cemetery after that night. Refused to sleep without a light on for the rest of his life.

A Warning in Granite

Groundskeepers won't go near the mausoleum after dark. One quit entirely after unlocking it for a family inspection and hearing footsteps scrape the stone floor—despite the chamber being empty and sealed. They say the door gets cold even in summer. Frost will form around its hinges in July.

And once, on a windless night, a visitor found their own breath fogging the glass of a nearby headstone… While the air around them stayed warm.

If you go to Riverside and find yourself in front of that forgotten vault, do not knock. And if you do—don't wait to hear what answers!

Ohio: Feu-Follet —Tiny Lights Beckon at Goll Woods

A Forest That Never Forgot

Tucked deep in the remains of the Great Black Swamp lies Goll Woods—a mosquito-choked patch of forest where the trees rise like black pillars and the air never seems to move. The lights appear in the quiet dark when the wind dies, and the leaves stop rustling.

They drift low along the ground, glowing softly—blue, green, and pale yellow. At first, they seem like fireflies or marsh gas.

But they do not flicker. They dance. Locals say they have minds of their own.

The Goll Family and the Land That Watched

In 1836, Peter and Catherine Goll brought their family from France and settled near this tract of land. They farmed, they built, and they buried their dead in the nearby clearing.

And even then, the lights were seen—gliding near the trees just beyond the lantern's glow. Some say the Golls, deeply religious, feared them.

Others say they tried to appease them—planting flowers around the old graves, crossing themselves as they passed the edge of the woods, never speaking their names aloud. But the lights came anyway.

They lingered near the Goll homestead and cemetery, especially during Lent.

Especially when the ground was soft and wet.

Especially at night.

The Feu-Follet and the Unblessed Dead

French settlers had a name for such things—feu-Follet.

Wandering lights. The spirits of those who died unbaptized—most often infants—were lost between this world and the next, seeking warmth, recognition, or company.

And sometimes… revenge.

They beckon.

They tempt. They lure travelers from the path. And once you've seen them, you cannot look away.

Many who followed the lights in Goll Woods were found face-down in shallow water, their faces twisted in confusion, hands reaching for something that was no longer there.

Others were never found at all.

Where the Light Touches, the Path Ends

The old swamp is mostly gone now—drained and buried under farmland and road. But Goll Woods remains. And so do the lights.

Hikers report them even now, darting just out of reach, always deeper into the trees. Phones die. Compasses spin. The trails, clear by day, seem to vanish by dusk. One woman who walked the trail came out feeling mesmerized. "They wanted me to hold them," she said, appearing dazed.

If You See the Light, Don't Follow

Some say it's just fungi or insects. Bioluminescence. Nature's illusion.

But ask the older locals, and their voices drop.

They'll tell you there's something in those woods.

Something that hums low to itself.

Something that remembers who walks through its shadow.

And if you see the lights glimmer between the trees—no matter how gentle or beautiful—do not follow them.

Because they are not lost. But they want you to be.

And they're looking for you.

Ohio: The Moonville Brakeman—The Rails Remember the Dead

A Tunnel, a Town, and a Trail of Ghosts

The town of Moonville is long gone. All that remains is a lonely stretch of reclaimed abandoned track nearly swallowed by the woods, a crumbling tunnel carved through rock, and whispers that follow hikers when the wind dies. Once, during the coal boom of the 19th century, trains thundered through here. The work was brutal. The air was thick with smoke. Men clung to the sides of railcars with raw hands and frozen breath.

And above it all, on the roofs of moving trains, walked the brakemen.

The Job That Took Men Apart

In those early days of the railroad, trains didn't slow easily. Brakemen were the ones who did the work—climbing up ladders, leaping between cars in motion, and turning rusted wheels in driving rain, snow, or wind.

It was dangerous.

Men lost their footing and fell between the cars.

Others were decapitated when they failed to duck in time beneath tunnels like the one at Moonville.

They worked drunk. They worked dead tired. Some didn't live long enough to learn from their mistakes.

The Man Who Slept on the Rails

One brakeman, headed home one damp night, stumbling along the line between Zaleski and Moonville.

He clutched a bottle of whiskey like it was a compass.

With every step, he drank. With every sip, he sagged.

The forest breathed around him—wet, black, and quiet. The tunnel loomed ahead. But he didn't make it.

He laid down instead. Rails for a pillow. Track for a bed. And sometime before the sun rose, a train roared through the dark and took off his head.

His skull bounced down into the ravine below, lost to the flood-swollen waters of a creek.

His body landed neatly in the brush, legs crossed like he'd gone peacefully. The bottle, miraculously intact, spun once in the center of the rails and came to rest without spilling more than a drop.

The Voice That Warned

At dawn, with rain still falling, a miner walking to the Zaleski mines spotted the bottle glinting between the rails.

He bent down to claim the prize.

Just as his fingers touched the glass, a voice scraped out from the fog:

"That's mine."

The miner froze. He looked left. Right. No one.

Then, blood. Small, dark specks on the stones.

He followed the trail over the rail bed and into the thicket where the ballast gave way to brush—and parted the leaves with trembling hands.

There, curled neatly between root and stone, was the headless body of the brakeman.

Still clutching nothing. Still bleeding something.

The Head That Was Never Found

The miner fled, screaming back to Moonville as thunder cracked overhead.

A party returned with shovels and lanterns. They buried the body beside the tracks.

But they never found the head.

Searchers combed the ravine. They waded Raccoon Creek even as it spilled over its banks in the storm.

But the brakeman's skull was gone—swept into the earth or stolen by something older than the rails.

The bottle remained.

And that… became the problem.

The Bottle No One Can Keep

The whiskey bottle sat in the same place on the tracks for years. Occasionally, someone would try to pick it up.

The voice would come each time just as their hand brushed the glass.

Raspy. Angry. Closer than it should be: "That's mine."

Fingers would recoil. Faces would drain pale.

Some dropped the bottle and ran.

Others claimed they felt a cold hand grip their wrist—something headless, something blind, but not lost.

No one kept the bottle for long.

But still, it sits there.

Waiting.

Walk Softly Past the Tunnel

Today, hikers walk the old Moonville rail trail, crossing the bridge and passing through the tunnel, never knowing what sleeps just beneath the ballast stones.

Some say if you stop near the tracks at dusk, you'll see the glint of a bottle.

Some say if you bend to touch it, you'll hear the gravel shift behind you.

And some say, if you listen long enough, you'll hear a voice—low, wet, and broken—call out from the dark with finality:

"That's mine."

Oklahoma: Dead Woman Crossing— A Bridge Cries Out

The Sound Beneath the Bridge

If you walk along the old road at dusk, just past where Deer Creek winds beneath the bridge, you might hear it.

The slow, rhythmic creak of wagon wheels.

A sharp rattle of harness leather.

And beneath it all, a woman's broken voice, drifting on the wind: "My baby… where is my baby?"

Locals know better than to stop. Because what

happened here was real. And what remains here is still listening.

A Woman Who Refused to Stay Silent

In the summer of 1905, Weatherford was a young, bustling town—its farms fertile, its tracks humming with trains from the Choctaw, Oklahoma, and Gulf Railroad. The streets bustled with ranchers and settlers. But not everyone who walked them had pure intent.

Twenty-nine-year-old schoolteacher Katie DeWitt James had made up her mind. She would leave her husband, Martin Luther James, a man whose anger had become as common in their home as dust. In her divorce petition, Katie recalled a night when Luther raised a chair above her head and snarled, "You ought to die. I have a notion to brain you with this chair."

On July 1st, 1905, drunk and furious, he stormed into their home again. Katie grabbed her infant daughter, Lula Blanche, and fled to her father's homestead. Six days later, she boarded a train bound for Weatherford, intending to travel to Ripley.

She was never seen alive again.

The Woman in the Buggy

When days passed, and no word came, Katie's father, Henry DeWitt, grew frantic. His daughter never arrived in Ripley. She had vanished.

The local sheriff could offer no answers. So, Henry hired private investigator Sam Bartell, who quickly uncovered a name that sent a chill through town: Fannie Norton. A laundress with three children, a bad reputation, and too many secrets.

Katie had met Fannie on the train. Witnesses saw them leave together. They stayed the night at a hotel owned by Fannie's sister. The next morning, the two women—and baby Lula—climbed into a buggy and headed down Dead Woman Road.

They were never seen together again.

Blood in the Blanket

A farmer near Deer Creek later reported something strange. A buggy pulled up, driven by a woman. She called to his young son and asked him to deliver a message to his mother: "Watch over the child. I'll be back soon."

She drove a short distance down the road… and hurled a bundle wrapped in a child's blanket into the weeds. When the farmer's wife opened it, she screamed. The baby's clothes were soaked in blood.

Fannie Norton was found days later in Shawnee. Brought in for questioning, she denied everything. Then, in the jail's toilet room, she swallowed poison.

Her last words were never heard.

Bones Beside the Water

It wasn't until August 31st, nearly two months after Katie vanished that G.W. Cornell stepped out of his buggy along the banks of Deer Creek and noticed something white in the grass.

A human skull—jaw still clenched in silence, a bullet hole bored clean through the temple. Katie's skeleton lay scattered nearby. A revolver. A tangle of clothing. Matted hair half-buried in the mud.

Her father identified her remains. The creek where she died was renamed Dead Woman Crossing.

Her killer was never brought to justice. Some whispered it was Luther James. He inherited custody of Lula Blanche. But even that ended in sorrow. At age eight, Lula died of spinal meningitis.

The Haunting That Remains

Today, hikers along the old trail say the wagon still rides that road.

They hear the hooves.

They hear the wheels.

They hear *her*.

Sometimes it's a whisper. Sometimes, a scream.

"Where is my baby?"

Others have reported a woman in white standing in the middle of the bridge, her dress wet, her arms outstretched.

When you blink—she's gone.

And if you listen closely, just beneath the creek's murmur, you might hear the voice of Katie DeWitt James, still searching.

Still calling. Still refusing to be forgotten.

Oregon: The Gray Lady of Heceta Head, Oregon Coast

Where the Fog Never Lifts

Perched high above the jagged Pacific cliffs, the Heceta Head Lighthouse has watched over the Oregon Coast since 1894. It is a beautiful tower painted in white, black, and red, with a keeper's house attached.

Its beam slices through rolling fog and salt-laced wind, warning ships of the rocky chaos below.

But sometimes, the light isn't enough.

The Toll Beneath the Waves

Over the years, ships have shattered against the reefs. They lie just beyond the cliffs. Their names are mostly forgotten. Their crews are not.

Survivors spoke of wind that changed direction in an instant. Waves that rose when the sea was calm.

Screams in the spray.

Bodies were pulled ashore, torn and bloated. Others were never recovered—dragged into the undertow and pulled into the black hollows of the Pacific.

Even the cliffs have claimed victims. Hikers straying too close to the edge vanished beneath the roar of waves, their final cries lost in the wind.

The House Beside the Light

For years, lighthouse keepers lived in the residence just beyond the tower—solitary lives wrapped in routine and silence. But that house, too, has stories it refuses to give up. They say a Woman in Gray walks the upper floors, her skirt whispering along the floorboards like mist through the grass. Doors slam without warning. Cabinets open. And on especially still nights, you might hear soft weeping from a room that hasn't had a bed in it for half a century. One keeper quit in the middle of the night after seeing a face in the mirror behind him that wasn't his own.

The Unmarked Grave

Not far from the lighthouse, hidden among ferns on a steep hillside, lies a single grave with no name. Locals believe it belongs to a woman—the gray figure still seen drifting the halls. Others think it's a sailor. Or a child.

The grave has been there as long as the lighthouse itself. Some say longer.

Flowers never grow there. No animals tread across it.

And those who walk near it feel watched—not with malice, but mourning.

The Wisps That Wander

People who visit Heceta Head today sometimes glimpse more than they bargained for. Pale figures drifting across the rocky bluffs. Wisps of smoke that move against the wind.

A woman in a gray skirt is seen from the waist down, vanishing just beyond the edge of the frame.

One photographer snapped a picture of the lighthouse at sunset. When she developed the film, dozens of faces pressed against the inside of the tower windows stared back at her. There had been no one inside.

Where the Light Still Turns

The Heceta Head Lighthouse is still active—still sweeping the waves with its beam. But not everything it shines on is alive.

The dead are still there—pulled by memory, salt, and sorrow.

And the woman in the gray skirt?

She walks the halls and hills, calling for something no one can hear. Or something no one should.

And in the fog, if you walk too far from the path… you may find that the light turns away.

And something else finds you instead.

Pennsylvania: The Bullet That Found Jennie Wade—Gettysburg

The Girl Who Never Left the Kitchen

She was only twenty. Her name was Mary Virginia "Jennie" Wade, and when the Battle of Gettysburg thundered into the streets, she wasn't hiding.

She was kneading bread dough in her sister's kitchen—her hands coated in flour, her sleeves rolled to the elbow. Her sister had just given birth. The baby cried upstairs.

Outside, the sky cracked with cannon fire. Rifle shots punched holes through homes.

But Jennie stayed.

She baked for Union soldiers, refusing to cower, her back turned to the window.

On the morning of July 3, 1863, a single bullet tore through the wooden door. It struck Jennie in the back, ripped through her shoulder, and buried itself in her heart.

She collapsed into the dough.

The bread never rose.

But her ghost did.

The House That Bled

Jennie's blood-soaked the floorboards where she fell.

Her mother screamed. Her sister fainted.

The baby kept crying.

They wrapped Jennie's body in a quilt and carried her upstairs, laying her beside the infant she had been helping protect.

The walls of the house still bear the scar: A jagged bullet hole through the door, a grim reminder of how far death can reach. And some say how long it can linger.

The Ghost Who Screams for Mercy

The house is a museum now. Tourists walk the same halls. They take pictures in front of the bullet-pierced door. They ask questions in hushed tones. But some get more than they came for. Visitors report a woman's scream, sharp and sudden, echoing through the house long after nightfall.

Not a moan. Not a whisper.

A scream of someone who didn't know she was dying.

Others say they've seen flour prints on the counter—cold and fresh—though no dough has been made there in over a hundred years. And if you stand in the kitchen too long, some claim you'll feel a hand press gently against your spine—right where the bullet passed through Jenny.

Baltimore Street Doesn't Sleep

Outside, on the street where Jennie's blood once ran in the dirt, people have seen her.

A young woman in a dark dress walks toward the house.

Head down.

Arms crossed.

Moving silently toward the place where her life ended and her legend began.

They say she disappears at the door.

And sometimes, they say, she screams first.

Rhode Island: Where Poe Knocked and Never Left

The Garden That Breathes in Silence

On 88 Benefit Street, in the shadow of St. John's Cathedral, where gravestones lean toward the earth as if listening, there sits a garden that never truly dies. At its heart stands the bold red house of Sarah Helen Whitman—widow, spiritualist, and poet of strange obsessions. In that garden, she once grew roses so pale they seemed to glow. Some say she spoke to them.

Some say they spoke back.

A Midnight Courtship

Here, under a full moon in July of 1845, Edgar Allan Poe first saw her.

Whitman moved through the rose garden like a figure in a dream—white gown trailing in the dew, silver scissors in her gloved hand, her eyes fixed on a blossom that refused to open.

Poe, walking alone, glimpsed her across the iron fence.

He later claimed the roses turned toward her, drawn by something not altogether human. They met. They corresponded. They nearly wed.

But something in their bond frayed before it bloomed.

She broke the engagement. He drank. He died.

And she never married again.

Where Roses Should Not Bloom

Visitors to the house—now private, though the garden remains visible from the street—have reported strange happenings. Roses that bloom in winter.

Footsteps on the gravel path when no one is there. And most disturbingly, a woman in white drifted through the rows, pausing now and then to snip the air with invisible shears. It is always around midnight.

And always under a full moon. Some passersby report hearing soft poetry whispered in the dark, the words never written by Poe or anyone living.

The Glow Behind the Window

At night, lights appear in the windows of the house. Some see two figures standing inside, shadowed and unmoving.

Others say they see just one: a woman with pale hair, her face turned not toward the garden but to the graveyard below.

That's where she said she wanted to be buried—among the dead, near Poe. But she never was. She lies elsewhere. And yet her spirit returns to this house.

The Roses That Feed on the Dead

One local groundskeeper tending nearby plots at St. John's claimed to find rose roots pushing up from underground—from nowhere near the garden.

They twisted between bones. Cracked through buried caskets. And when one root was cut, it bled. A pale pink, like watered wine.

That same week, someone plucked a rose from the Whitman garden and brought it home. Within days, every mirror in their home reflected her, not them.

The Twist of the Shears

Here's the truth no one wants to say out loud: Sarah Helen Whitman didn't just mourn Poe. She bound him.

Some believe the rose garden was never meant to honor him—but to trap him. And when the full moon rises and the air grows wet with rot, she walks again—clipping roses, whispering spells, and calling softly:

"You may go... when I do." But she hasn't.

And neither has he. So, if you walk by the garden under moonlight and you hear a soft snip behind you—don't turn around. Because she might be pruning again.

And this time, you might be the bloom that Poe wasn't.

South Carolina: Murrells Inlet– Where Love Rots in the Marsh

The Girl Who Loved the Wrong Man

They say she was beautiful.

Alice Flagg, just fifteen, lived at The Hermitage on the Grand Strand, where the marsh never sleeps, and the ocean air carries old secrets inland. Her family wanted power. Position. A marriage to wealth.

But Alice fell in love with John Braddock, a poor lumberman who smelled of pine and promise.

Their love was hidden beneath fabric and expectation—a simple gold ring—tied to a blue ribbon, worn tight around her neck, pressed against her heart.

She never took it off. Until they made her.

The Man Who Took Everything

When her brother, Doctor Allard, discovered the romance, he sent her away to Charleston—to a boarding school surrounded by strangers and salt-soaked stone.

Far from John. Far from the only thing that made her feel alive. She withered in that place. Her letters were intercepted.

The ring remained hidden—her last tether to love.

But the Lowcountry is no place to mourn. Malaria came. It soaked her fevered body and twisted her dreams.

She slipped into a coma and never woke up.

Before she died, Doctor Allard removed the ribbon from her throat. He ripped the ring away and flung it into the creek like filth. He believed she'd survive.

She didn't.

The Grave That Knows

They buried her at All Saints Waccamaw Episcopal Cemetery beneath a plain, cold slab.

It bears no name—only "Alice."

But the grave remembers. It holds what the ring once did. Grief. Betrayal. Unrest. Visitors who linger hear scratching beneath the stone.

Some have seen a pale girl rise from the ground in a soaked nightgown, clutching her throat, gasping—searching for something she can no longer wear.

The Ritual They Regret

They say if you walk backward around Alice's grave 13 times under a full moon… and leave a ring behind, *she will come for it.*

But don't mistake her for the lovesick child they buried. She comes twisted now.

Gaunt.

Wet.

Hair matted with grave dirt and weeds.

And her hands shake—not with longing, but rage.

Those who have seen her say she doesn't speak.

She points to her chest.

To the scar where the ribbon once lay.

Then she screams.

The Ring That Still Calls Her

Sometimes, rings vanish from the grave.

Other times, they're found bent, rusted—sunken into the earth like they tried to crawl away.

Locals whisper that if you listen near the old marsh, you can hear the drag of bare feet in the grass, the rasp of ribbon against bone.

And if you feel cold, fingers brush your throat…don't look down.

Because she may be trying to see if you're the one who took her ring.

Or worse—if you're still wearing yours.

South Dakota: Broken Boot Gold Mine—The Dead are not so Dead

What Was Buried Should Have Stayed Buried

The Broken Boot Gold Mine, nestled just outside the lawless sprawl of historic Deadwood, opened in 1878 and was founded by Olaf Seim and James Nelson. Back then, it was just another hole in the Black Hills—scraped into the side of a mountain, fueled by desperation and the dream of gold.

They called it Seim's Mine at first. Men had already died in the dark by the time it was renamed.

From 1878 to 1904, miners dug day and night, carving veins of gold and iron from beneath the hills. It reopened briefly during World War I, feeding the hungry jaws of war with iron and sulfur for munitions. But when the war ended in 1918, the tunnels were sealed, the lamps were snuffed out, and the mountain was left to its silence.

Or so they thought.

The town forgot the mine.

But the mine did not forget them.

The Breathing That Never Stops

Today, the Broken Boot Mine is just another tourist stop—daily tours, dusty souvenirs, scripted history.

But not all the guides follow the script.

Some whisper about the breathing. It starts near the lowest shaft, where the walls close in tighter, and even the strongest lanterns seem to flicker for no reason. There's no airflow. No gaps in the rock. But the moment the tour group falls silent, you can hear it:

A slow, wet exhale.

Just behind you.

Waiting.

The Man Left Behind

The legend goes that in the early 1880s, a miner named Thomas was crushed in a tunnel collapse. The cave-in was so deep that no one could reach him.

They sealed the shaft and said prayers.

But the other miners kept hearing things. Knocks on the timber supports. Tools tapping in the dark. Whispers.

They joked that Thomas was still working his shift.

Until one man didn't come back. And then another.

That shaft has remained closed for over a century. But things still move behind the boards.

"Don't Move."

Visitors have reported tools going missing, only to be found later—standing upright on their handles like someone pushed them through solid stone.

One guide tells of a woman who wandered from the group. She thought she saw a man in the distance—bent, limping, holding a lantern that glowed too dim, too cold.

She followed. She was found curled in the corner of the tunnel, her eyes wide, hands pressed over her ears.

All she kept saying was: "He told me not to move."

Something Works the Night Shift

Those who work the mine know the signs:

Dust disturbed with no footprints. Shadows cast where no one stands. Rusted rails that hum like something's riding them. And always, the exact phrase whispered in the black: "Stay back. Stay down."

It's not a warning. It's a memory. A voice trying to keep you from dying like he did—trapped between earth and iron, bones splintered, lungs filling with dust.

But not even death could clock him out.

The Sealed Shaft Bleeds

The lowest shaft is blocked by rotting boards and rusted bolts. Sometimes, scratches appear on the inside.

Thin and frantic. Like nails. Like he's still trying to dig out. Or drag someone in.

One guide swore he saw a lantern light behind the barrier. When he looked closer, he saw Thomas's face in the reflection—just his face.

Upside down.

If You Hear Breathing, Don't Run

Some things in Broken Boot never stopped working.

Some spirits, like the machinery they ran, just keep turning.

So, if you ever find yourself in the mine— and the air grows still and your light begins to flicker and you hear a slow breath near your shoulder…

Don't move.

Because Thomas is there.

Still watching.

Still waiting.

And if you make a sound… he might not be able to tell you from the rock.

Tennessee: The Ghost of Roaring Forks, Great Smoky Mountains

The Barefoot Girl on the Trail

It was a sharp-breathed autumn night in the early 1900s when a young man named Foster rode horseback along the old road that traced the Roaring Fork stream. The moon hung low, pale, and heavy, casting silver light across the darkened hollows and whispering trees. The only sounds were the hooves beneath him and the restless murmuring of the creek beside the trail.

He saw her as he passed through the quiet folds of Spruce Flats, where mist clung low to the earth, and cabins lay scattered like broken teeth.

A girl.

She appeared on the road without warning—standing barefoot, wearing a thin white muslin gown that clung to her skin in the cool night air. Her hair hung damp and tangled, and Foster saw, with a strange certainty, that she was not afraid.

She did not speak; she only lifted her chin as though waiting.

Foster, startled but kind, offered her a place on his horse.

She climbed into the saddle behind him, and as the horse moved, he caught the scent of wood smoke in her hair—as if she had been sitting by a hearth that had long since gone cold.

The Fire Still Burns

They rode in silence, moonlight falling across the trail.

But just before the crossing near the deeper bend in the creek, the girl grabbed the reins and pulled hard. The horse reared slightly, and before Foster could speak, she leapt down and vanished into the trees—bare feet barely touching the leaves.

Foster sat frozen. He waited, watching the place where she had disappeared. Then, unnerved but unsure why, he turned toward his cabin and rode into the hills. But her image stayed with him—the smoke, the gown, the silence. And before the fire in his own hearth had died down, he found himself riding back.

The Door That Waited

He followed the same trail, letting the sound of the creek guide him. Soon, tucked among the trees, he saw a second cabin—modest, hand-built, with light flickering faintly through the seams of the door.

He approached and raised his hand to knock.

The door opened before he touched it.

An elderly couple stood inside—faces hollow, eyes sunken from time and sorrow. Foster stammered a greeting. He told them what he'd seen, of the barefoot girl in white, of the scent of smoke, and how she had leapt from his horse and vanished into the woods.

The old man's hand trembled at the edge of the doorframe. "That would be our daughter, Lucy," he said. And Foster felt the cold seep down his spine. "She's been dead ten years now."

The Ghost of the Creek

They told him the truth. Lucy died in a fire—their cabin by the creek had caught flame one bitter winter's night. They had escaped. She had not.

Her body was never recovered. Only the scorched bones of her bedframe and the blue glass beads she wore around her wrist.

They could not bear to remain near the place where she burned, so they rebuilt farther up the creek in silence and sorrow.

"But sometimes," the man said, barely audible, "when the moon is right… and someone rides the road at night… she follows. She's always looking. Maybe for us."

She Still Waits

Since that night, others have seen her, too.

Travelers along the Roaring Fork Motor Nature Trail have reported a girl in white waving from the edge of the woods or standing still beside the road, barefoot, her head tilted in quiet anticipation.

Sometimes, she disappears before you stop.

Sometimes, if you do, she climbs in silently.

A few claim to have ridden several minutes before noticing the air behind them grow impossibly cold and the scent of old wood smoke drifting into their lungs.

Others have looked into their rearview mirror only to see nothing at all.

Just an empty seat.

And a faint impression—like someone had been sitting there.

If You See Lucy

If you're driving the trail under a Smoky Mountain moon, and you see a pale figure lift her hand toward you…think carefully.

She doesn't want a ride.

She wants to be remembered.

She wants to come home.

And some say she brings the fire with her.

Tennessee: The Bell Witch—Where the Devil Came to Visit

A Curse in the Crooked Ground

In the early 1800s, John Bell brought his family to a stretch of fertile land in the Red River settlement of Robertson County, Tennessee. It should have been a beginning. Instead, it was an invitation.

The land was old. The trees bent strangely. The air hung too still at dusk. In 1817 something came to the Bell farm—not seen, but deeply felt. It crept in with the night. It lingered in the rafters. And it never came alone.

The Thing That Watched

At first, it was subtle. John Bell reported seeing a creature in the field—a dog's body with the head of a rabbit, its eyes like rotting marbles, its mouth chewing something it hadn't caught.

The family began to hear knocking on the walls—fists pounding from the inside.

The beds creaked with gnawing sounds, as if rats were chewing through the wood, though no holes were ever found.

Growls echoed from the corners.

Sometimes, they heard each other's voices coming from empty rooms.

But it wasn't them.

It was something pretending.

Betsy and the Voice of Kate

Betsy Bell, the youngest daughter, was the first to bleed. She woke with bruises across her face, the shape of fingers too large for a human hand.

She was slapped, scratched, and thrown from her bed, her screams muffled by some force that seemed to enjoy the sound of it.

The spirit soon spoke. It named itself "Kate" and claimed to be the ghost—or worse—of a neighbor, Kate Batts, long rumored to dabble in dark arts and local vengeance.

It mocked the family in sing-song voices.

It mimicked the dead. It knew what they feared.

And it grew stronger the more they suffered.

The House That Could Not Sleep

Sheets were ripped from the children while they slept.

Chairs scraped across the floors by unseen hands.

The Bible was torn apart.

Fireplaces roared to life without flame. Visitors came to witness the haunting—and left broken, white-haired with terror. Betsy began to lose time. She'd fall unconscious for hours, wake screaming with bite marks on her arms.

No one could stop it. No one could help her.

The Death of John Bell

In 1820, the entity turned its attention fully to John Bell.

It whispered to him in his sleep. It told him he would die. "December 20," it hissed. "December 20."

That morning, he was found writhing, his tongue blackened. Beside his bed lay a vial of dark liquid no one could identify.

The spirit laughed when they found it. "I gave him that," it said. "He'll never wake up again."

He didn't.

They burned the vial, but the smell never left the house.

It's Never Really Gone

After John's death, the torment slowed.

The voices grew faint.

The sounds faded.

But the house rotted in silence, and the land grew cold.

They said the Bell Witch had finished her task. But sometimes, people still hear whispers in the fields. Or feel fingers brush their cheek when no one is near. Children who sleep near Red River wake choking, whispering the name "Kate." Sometimes, a dark shape walks along the edge of the trees—half woman, half shadow, head tilted like she's listening.

If You Hear Her Knock

The ruins are gone, but the ground remembers.

And if you're in Robertson County late at night and hear a knock at the door or a low voice calling your name from just behind the wall—Don't answer.

It is too late.

She's already inside.

And she so wants to torment you.

Texas: The Hollow That Won't Let Go

A Pretty Place with Bad Bones

Lindsey Hollow Road curls beneath the trees like a noose—winding through Cameron Park, where the Brazos River cuts deep, and the hills rise like grave mounds. It is beautiful by daylight. But under the moon, it is *different*. In the 1870s and 1880s, this land was no place for peace. Horse thieves and cattle rustlers roamed like wolves in human skin, always moving, always watching. Justice, when it came, wasn't through trial. It came with rope. With bullets.

With men who didn't wear badges but swung judgment anyway.

The Brothers Who Didn't Stay Buried

The story says two brothers—the Lindseys—ran horses stolen from ranchers, hiding them in the brush near the Brazos.

Their name turned to curse.

Their faces were feared.

But one night, the wrong rancher followed their tracks too far. He caught them near the banks.

No sheriff. No warning.

Just gunpowder and rage.

The fight was fast. One Lindsey brother died screaming into the river. The other was dragged from the road—half-dead, still bleeding—and buried in a shallow grave just beyond the tree line.

Too shallow. Too fast. Too late.

The Grave That Opens at Night

They say the earth rejected him. The grave split open days later as if something inside had clawed upward, not down. And after that… things changed.

Travelers along Lindsey Hollow began hearing moaning in the trees—low and animal-like. Lights flickered across the trail where no lanterns could be.

Horses refused to cross the creek.

Dogs howled until their throats were raw.

Some saw a figure—head low, arms bent the wrong way, walking the edge of the riverbank.

Always wet. Always watching.

The Spirit Along the Brazos

The ghost of the buried brother doesn't speak. He groans like a dying man who still wants to kill. Sometimes, hikers in Cameron Park feel their shoulders tugged as they pass the hollow.

Others say they saw a face in the creek, staring up through the water, mouth full of mud, as if waiting to be pulled out—or pull someone in.

They say he wants vengeance.

Or perhaps he wants to switch places.

And on nights when the wind cuts hard through the hillocks and the flickering lights return, locals know to stay away from the path. Because if you see the figure on the trail and he turns toward you—it means he remembers.

If You Walk the Hollow

Lindsey Hollow Road still lies beneath the trees, open to the curious.

But the ground there doesn't forget.

And if you hear dragging steps behind you or feel cold breath on the back of your neck—*don't turn around.*

Because if you do, you might find a very bad man who was never properly buried…and is still looking for a grave deep enough.

Or someone to blame for his death.

Texas: Ghost Road

Ghost Road

Deep in the pine woods near Saratoga, Texas, there is a stretch of dirt road called Bragg Road—though most don't call it that anymore. They call it Ghost Road.

Nearly eight miles of winding trail swallowed in trees and thick brush, where the light never quite feels like sunlight. Where silence falls heavy, and the road seems to stretch farther the longer you walk it. It was once a railroad spur—laid down in 1901 during the roaring East Texas oil boom. A profitable lifeline for timber and labor.

A straight-shot line to nowhere, ending in trees that never stopped growing.

By 1934, the tracks were torn up, and the trains long gone. But something still walks the line.

The Lantern in the Pines

Since the early 1900s, travelers along Bragg Road have reported a light—distant, bobbing, always just out of reach. Sometimes it's white. Other times, blood red.

It drifts between the trees like it knows the path better than you do. And if you chase it, it vanishes. Some claim it's swamp gas or headlights refracted through the trees.

But the locals know better.

They say it's the spirit of a railroad worker, killed one night while walking the tracks with his lantern. No one knows why he was out there. But the story goes: he never saw the train. And the train never slowed.

The Search That Never Ends

His body was found broken and scattered. But his head was never recovered. Since then, the light has returned—again and again. Always along the old track line. Always swinging slow, side to side, like a lantern held in an unsteady hand.

They say the ghost is still searching. For his head. For the train.

For the last moment, he remembers.

And if you stand on Bragg Road long enough, you may see the light approaching. But be warned:

If the light stops— If it flickers and grows brighter—

It means it's looking at you.

Where the Trees Breathe

Even in daylight, Bragg Road feels wrong.

No birds sing. The pines creak softly as though something large moves between them. Footsteps echo louder than they should. Some who have visited the road say they felt watched—not from the woods, but from above as if something were pacing silently along the branches.

And a few have seen the light begin behind them, growing brighter as they ran.

If You See the Light

The Ghost Road is open. You can visit it today.

You might see nothing at all.

Or you might see the faint glow of a lantern far down the road—swinging gently, side to side, in the rhythm of footsteps that haven't stopped in over a hundred years.

And if you follow it…

Just be sure you don't look away.

Because some say the worker's body was buried nearby.

But his head?

He still cannot find it.

Utah: White Lady of Spring Canyon

A Town Built on Coal and Bone

The town once called Storrs—later known as Spring Canyon—was carved into the black hills of Carbon County, Utah, in the early 20th century.

It promised progress. Paychecks. Firelight in every window. But the only thing deeper than the coal seams was the death that came with them.

Founded in 1912, the Spring Canyon Coal Company, backed by Jesse Knight and other investors, dug greedily into the mountains. The town grew quite suddenly.

Rows of miner's homes, a schoolhouse, shops, and even a swimming pool. By 1924, it was thriving.

But coal towns like Spring Canyon always thrived on the edge of a grave. The mines were deep. The dust choked. And death came often without ceremony—a cave-in, a fire, a breath too many of black air.

The Widow of Latuda

Not far from Spring Canyon, in the smaller settlement of Latuda, a woman waited for her husband to return from his shift. He never did. His body was never recovered—swallowed whole by the mine.

A tomb with no marker. No goodbyes.

She was left with two children and no income. In desperation, she went to the mine bosses. She begged. Pleaded. They gave her nothing. Not even coal to warm her hands.

Her grief turned inward. Her mind fractured.

One freezing night, she led her children to the creek. And she held them under—until they no longer kicked.

Until the water ran quiet.

She vanished into the hills and, days later, was found wandering Salt Lake City in a stupor.

She was committed to an asylum. But her screams kept returning to Spring Canyon.

The Return

Years later, she escaped.

No one knows how she made it back to the canyon—gaunt, wild-eyed, half-shadow. But one night, a lantern was seen flickering near the old mine mouth.

Miners who remained went to look. They found her hanging from a collapsed timber, just above the spot where her husband was believed to have died. They buried her beside the mine, beneath a rock no one marked. *But she did not stay buried.*

The Woman in White

Since her death, something has moved in the ruins of Spring Canyon.

Locals and hikers have reported a woman in a white dress, wet and clinging, wandering the canyon wash and the mine entrances, her head tilted toward the dark shafts, listening. She is never seen by day.

Only after sunset, when the wind picks up, and the trees begin to creak.

Some hear her singing lullabies just before nightfall.

Others have followed the sound of a child crying— only to find the stream perfectly still. And those who venture too close to the mine mouth at night sometimes see small, wet footprints leading toward the water.

Then… nothing.

If You See Her

They say she still searches for her children. Or for the husband she never got to bury. Or maybe she's waiting to pull someone else into the black with her—to make someone feel what she did. And if you see her—if you catch the pale drift of her gown near the edge of the mine or the creek— Don't follow. Because she is not lost.

She's waiting. And she remembers what was taken from her. Now she takes back.

Vermont: The Grave with a Window

Here lies the Body

Beneath a weathered concrete slab on Town Hill Road at Evergreen Cemetery in New Haven lies the body of Timothy Clark Smith, buried in 1893 with a bell in his hand and a glass window over his face—just in case he wasn't dead. *He feared being buried alive.*

They say if you visit his grave at dusk and lean close to the ground, you might hear it—the faint sound of a bell ringing beneath the earth. And if you do…don't look in the window. Because sometimes, someone looks back.

Vermont: The Devil's Footprints of Glastenbury Mountain

A Mountain That Doesn't Forget

High in the wilds of southwestern Vermont rises Glastenbury Mountain, a place long avoided by the native Abenaki people, who warned of an "evil wind" that swept down its slopes. They refused to hunt there. Refused to linger after dusk. By the late 1800s, settlers ignored the warnings. A few logging and mining communities sprang up along the ridges, including the now-abandoned town of Glastenbury itself.

But strange things began to happen.

People began disappearing.

The Bennington Triangle

Between 1945 and 1950, five people vanished in the forests near Glastenbury Mountain without a trace. Among them:

Paula Welden, a college student who went for a hike in 1946 and was never seen again.

James Tetford, a veteran who vanished from a bus—his belongings left behind on his seat.

A boy, a woman, a hiker—all vanished the same way: no signs of struggle, no bodies, no clues.

Locals began calling it the *Bennington Triangle*, but some say the disappearances started long before that.

There's a legend that dates back to the early 1800s, told in whispers by loggers and hunters, about a man who followed a trail of odd prints in the snow—hoof-like but walking on two legs.

He was never seen again.

The Prints That Don't Melt

Old logbooks kept by early settlers describe a storm in 1855, after which strange prints appeared in the snow around the edges of the mountain—cloven, deep, and spaced like something walking upright. They crossed over fences without breaking the rails. They stopped beside windows.

And then vanished at the edge of the trees.

Those who followed them into the woods never returned.

Those who stayed behind heard knocking at their doors in the night— but no one ever stood outside.

The Spirit in the Stone Circle

Near the summit of Glastenbury Mountain lies a stone circle, overgrown and half-buried in moss. Hikers who've stumbled upon it report sudden nausea, blackouts, or a strange loss of time—as if hours vanished in the blink of an eye.

One man reported standing inside the circle when everything went silent—no birds, no wind. When he turned to leave, he saw footprints behind him.

They weren't his. And they led right into the center of the circle… and stopped.

If You Hike Glastenbury

The area is still open to hikers, though the old town is gone, swallowed by forest. But those who go deep into the woods sometimes hear voices—soft, like someone calling their name from behind a tree. Others report seeing flickering lantern lights, but when they follow them, they find only emptiness.

And some never make it back at all.

Locals say if you see strange prints in the snow… don't follow them.

And if the woods fall silent around you—run.

Because whatever haunts Glastenbury Mountain doesn't like to be seen.

And it's always looking for someone to take.

Virginia: Sarver Shelter

They Lived in a Cabin

Henry and Sarah Sarver built their cabin beneath Sinking Creek Mountain in 1859. They lived—and died—in that hollow. Only ruins remain now.

But hikers who camp near the old homestead at Sarver Shelter report strange things: footsteps in the dark, whispers with no source, and hands shaking them awake at night. Some say if you hear rapping on the walls, don't open your eyes. Because something might be staring back!

Virginia: Bunny Man of Colchester Overpass

It Started with a Rabbit

In 1970, two people reported being attacked near the Southern Railway overpass by a man in a white rabbit costume—but this was no prank.

He carried a hatchet. He smashed windows.

He whispered about trespassers and blood.

Since then, others have seen him too—a chubby figure in a stained bunny suit, standing beneath the overpass.

He has a hatchet in his hand, watching.

They say if you're near Colchester Bridge after midnight, you might hear scraping along the guardrail, or find fresh claw marks in the concrete.

And if you see white ears in the dark—run.

Because the Bunny Man doesn't hop.

He hunts.

Washington: Fort Vancouver Gray Lady

The Fort That Watches Back

Fort Vancouver was built in the 1820s as a trading post for the Hudson's Bay Company. It later became a military stronghold; over the decades, it absorbed war, fire, famine, and rot into its walls. Thousands passed through its gates. Not all of them left. And some... never stayed dead. Of all the whispers that swirl around its crumbling foundations, none carry the weight of terror quite like the Gray Lady.

The Hospital That Still Hears

She is often seen in the old hospital building, now repurposed as a museum—but the structure remembers its purpose. It remembers the screams of soldiers burned in the fire, the coughing blood of those who died of disease, and the infants who never cried.

The staff says she moves like breath across the glass—silent, gliding, always just ahead, her footsteps ticking across the wooden floors in the dead of night.

Heels. Always heels. And then the air grows cold.

And the smell of lavender crawls into your lungs.

And the lights flicker in rooms with no electricity.

A Veil That Hides Nothing

Witnesses describe her in a long gray dress, shoulders hunched, veil hanging like cobwebs from her brow. Sometimes, she's seen rocking an infant in her arms, though the infant never makes a sound.

And on rare nights—when she pauses—someone sees her lift her veil. But there's nothing underneath.

No eyes. No mouth.

Just a black emptiness that stretches far, far too deep.

When She Follows You Home

One security guard quit after just three nights. He refused to speak of what he saw—until his wife told someone what he'd started doing: Laying towels outside their bedroom each night.

Trying to catch the wet footprints that appeared on the carpet. Just outside the door.

Every. Single. Night.

He never saw her in his home. But he heard her.

Click. Click. Click.

Like heels on wooden floors... where there was only carpet.

If You Smell Lavender

The Gray Lady doesn't haunt. She lingers.

Some say she was a nurse who died during the Fort's great fever outbreak.

Others say she was a mother searching for her child—still cradling the blanket long after her arms decayed.

But no one knows what happens when she finally finds what she's looking for.

So, if you're in Fort Vancouver, and the air turns cold, and the scent of lavender curls around your neck, don't look behind you.

She only comes when you notice.

And once she does...

she doesn't leave.

West Virginia: Lake Shawnee Amusement Park

The Land That Should Not Be Disturbed

Before the laughter. Before the rides.

Before the ticket booth rusted to dust.

There was blood.

In 1783, at the edge of the woods and near the banks of a slow-moving river, a young girl named Tabitha Clay fought to keep her brother's body from being scalped.

They were just children.

She was stabbed to death. Her brother, Bartley, was shot in the chest. Another son, Ezekiel, was dragged into the forest and burned alive.

The Clay children were buried in shallow earth.

The land was never quiet again. It would remember.

A Park Built Over Suffering

In 1926, long after the Clay family had vanished from memory, Conley Snidow, Sr. opened a children's amusement park on the very site where those first brutal deaths occurred.

A Ferris wheel. A swimming pool. A circle of swings.

The land tolerated it for a time. Then it began to bleed again.

In 1927, a young girl named Emiline Shrader—all bows and bright eyes—was playing on the swings when a truck backed over her. Witnesses say she never screamed. Her body hit the ground like a dropped doll.

Later, a boy named George Wythe drowned in the pool, pulled down by something no one could see—his body trapped, his limbs torn against the drain grates.

The laughter stopped. The rides slowed.

And soon, Lake Shawnee closed.

The Bones Beneath

In the 1980s, Gaylord White attempted to reopen the park. As bulldozers pushed into the earth, they struck something ancient. Bones. Hundreds of them.

Children's teeth. Small skulls. Beads and arrowheads are buried deep beneath the grass.

A forgotten Shawnee burial ground.

No one counted how many graves they unearthed before they stopped digging.

But by then, the spirits were already awake.

The Ghosts That Refused to Leave

The land changed after that. Visitors began seeing shadows moving beneath the trees. Swings would sway without wind. And laughter—children's laughter—would echo through the rusted skeletons of the rides long after dark. One man swore he saw a little girl in a blood-soaked dress watching from behind the swing set. When he turned to run, he heard the chains creak.

And the swing began to move.

If You Visit the Park

Lake Shawnee is abandoned now. But the Clay children are still buried there. So are the bones from centuries ago.

And so is something else—older than war, older than names, curled in the soil like a scream never finished.

Some say you can visit the grounds today. That it's just an old amusement park.

But others know better.

They say the blood never dried.

And if you step too close to the old swing set at dusk—

You'll hear it.

Not laughter.

Not weeping.

Just the slow creak of chains.

And then the sound of something moving in the dirt beneath you.

West Virgina: Booger Hole

A Name Earned in Blood

There's a place in northern Clay County, tucked deep in the Rush Fork Valley, where the trees grow too close, and the air turns heavy long before sundown.

They call it Booger Hole.

The name is older than memory; no one says it without a whisper. Because from the late 1800s to the early 1900s, something terrible stirred in that hollow—something that drank men's names and spat back bones.

Nearly a dozen people vanished or were murdered here. And none of them went quietly.

The Vanishing

In 1883, Andy Hargis, a stonemason, was last seen walking the road from Elana. His boots were found in the dirt. Nothing else.

In 1897, a traveling watchmaker, Joseph Clark, stayed overnight in Booger Hole. The next day, all that remained was a trail of blood leading into a swollen creek.

By 1899, the deaths were bolder.

Louis Cohen, a farmer, was found slaughtered in his own field. And Lacy Ann Boggs, a 74-year-old woman, was shot through the window while peeling apples in an abandoned schoolhouse she called home.

The townsfolk grew sick with fear. They stopped talking. Stopped asking. Until one day, they snapped.

The Mob's Fire

A mob formed—silent, furious.

They dynamited five homes belonging to those rumored to be behind the killings. Flames roared through the hollow. The accused were warned: leave or die.

They left. But something stayed behind.

The Babies in the Fire

The worst legend, the one whispered only after dark, is that of the woman in the cabin—the one who lived near the creek, hidden in rot and ivy.

They say she had many children.

But no one ever saw them. Only heard them.

Screaming.

Because every time she gave birth, she took the newborn and threw it into the fire.

And even after she died, the crying didn't stop.

People walking near the hollow say they hear it still—wet gasps, soft sobs, the sound of tiny fists pounding on blackened logs.

Some say you can see her shadow in the doorway, still rocking an empty cradle.

Still waiting for the silence that never comes.

If You Walk Booger Hole

Today, Booger Hole is quiet. The roads are rough. The trees have grown over the old cabins. But if you listen closely, you might hear:

The footsteps of the missing.

A gunshot in the wind.

A child's cry beneath your feet.

And if you see a light in the window of the ghost of the old schoolhouse—don't follow it.

Because the dead in Booger Hole don't rest.

They remember.

And worse—they want you to remember, too.

Wisconsin: Beast of Bray Road

Something Hunts in the Cornfields

Along the dark bends of Bray Road in Walworth County, something moves where headlights fade and stalks where the corn grows high.

It's not a man. And it's not a wolf.

But something inbetween—something older.

Reports of the Beast of Bray Road date back to 1936, the first of which came from St. Coletta School, where workers claimed to see a massive, fur-covered figure watching from the edge of the tree line.

Since then, it's never truly gone away. It just waits for the night.

Eyes in the Rearview Mirror

The creature is said to stand six to seven feet tall, hunched but powerful, with arms too long for its body and shoulders that roll like a man's. Its face is that of a wolf, but wrong—too expressive, too aware. The snout snarls back at the headlights.

And then there are the eyes—red, orange, and glowing like embers buried in ash.

Witnesses claim it walks like a man but runs like a beast, capable of dropping to all fours and galloping with terrifying speed. Those who see it never forget.

The Slash That Stayed

In the 1980s and 1990s, encounters surged. People began whispering again, locking doors they never used to lock. An infamous account came from Lori Endrizzi, who claimed the creature lunged at her car one night. She saw it standing in the road, illuminated only by their high beams. It didn't flinch. It waited.

And when she got too close, it leapt—its claws dragging down the length of the vehicle, leaving deep, unnatural gouges in the metal. There were no tracks. Just the marks. And a smear of something that looked too dark to be mud.

It Doesn't Want to Be Seen—Until It Does

Locals say the Beast of Bray Road moves mostly at dusk and dawn, between light and dark, between the things we know and pretend not to.

It's been seen crouching in fields.

Loping beside moving cars at impossible speed.

Even gnawing at roadkill with long, humanlike hands. Those who've encountered it speak of a strange sound—not a growl, but a wet, clicking breath, as if it's sniffing more than air.

And they always say the same thing:

It knew they were there.

And it wanted them to know it could've come closer.

If You Drive Bray Road

People still see it.

You can drive to Bray Road tonight if you'd like.

It's still there, winding past rusted silos and overgrown fields.

But if your headlights catch something tall…

and it doesn't move…

and it watches as you pass…

Don't stop. Don't slow down.

And whatever you do—don't look in the rearview mirror.

Because if you do…it might be running behind you.

Wisconsin: The Ridgeway Ghost

Along the Old Military Road Where the Dead Still Walk—A Trail of Lead and Blood

Between the crooked timber towns of Dodgeville and Blue Mounds, where wind scrapes the hills like fingernails on bone, the Old Military Road carved a trail of greed and death through the Wisconsin wilderness.

In the 1840s, lead miners came by the thousands.

They dug, drank, and died. Saloons outnumbered churches.

Graves outnumbered names.

And along this road—through a stretch of fog-wet woods and restless soil—something began to walk.

They called it the Ridgeway Ghost.

And it didn't just haunt.

It hunted.

The First Sightings: Riders and Hanging Trees

The first man to see it was a doctor, riding late through the night. He felt the chill first—a breath against his neck. Then he turned and saw a specter on the back of his horse, face dripping with rot, clinging like a corpse afraid of hell.

Not long after, Johnnie Owens, whistling his way down the trail, looked up and saw bodies hanging from the trees, necks twisted, tongues bloated.

When the sun rose, they were gone.

But Johnnie never sang again.

It Doesn't Speak—But It Follows

Jim Moore, just a man trying to walk home from his sweetheart's farm, felt a presence beside him—matching his steps, silent and cold. He turned and saw a figure, pale and grinning, walking shoulder-to-shoulder with him back to Pokerville.

They never spoke. Jim never went back to the farm.

And his sweetheart married someone else.

A Monster in the Brush

The Ridgeway Ghost became more than a presence.

It grew bold.

It leapt from the thick roadside brush onto passing buggies, snarling and screeching. Horses panicked.

Wagons flipped. Bones broke. Sometimes, it climbed into the seat beside the driver and threw them to the ground, laughing in a voice that wasn't made for laughter. And always—always—the air stank of sulfur and wet meat.

A wrestler once declared he would defeat the ghost.

He walked the road alone.

The next morning, they found his body mangled inside a fence, the ground torn up in circles as if something had slaughtered the man, gulped him down, and spit out the remains.

Then danced around the corpse.

The Ghost That Carries Tools

Even the oxen drivers, grim men used to death, learned to dread the stretch past Ridgeway.

John Riley stopped at a tavern for one drink. When he returned, his oxen were untied—but neatly tethered to the wagon. His whip and lantern were gone. He looked down the road and saw a crooked figure walking into the night with his tools, its back bent but its steps steady.

He left the load behind. He never took that road again.

It Lingers With the Dead

Even after the railroad came and the wagons stopped, the ghost lingered.

In the 1930s, Louis Meuer, a cemetery sexton, was found hanged in the shed beside the graves he tended. They said it was suicide. But the ground around his body was dragged in a spiral, like something had circled him.

Locals whispered: "He offended the Ridgeway Ghost."

What Is It? No one agrees on what it is.

Some say it's a miner crushed in the tunnels before the war.

Others say it's a peddler stabbed in a barroom brawl, buried beneath a tavern floor.

Most speak of the two brothers, one of whom was thrown into a fireplace during a fight—his skin peeled from the flames. The other shot dead.

They say the ghost is both brothers—merged, burned, and screaming. One soul, twice the rage.

If You See It

People still walk that road.

Some say it's safe now. Others know better.

If you feel the air change,

If you hear something in the brush,

If your car has a flat tire…

Don't stop.

Don't run.

Because the Ridgeway Ghost doesn't like fear.

It *loves* it.

And if it climbs into the seat beside you—don't look.

That's how it finds out your fears and it feeds on them.

And then, you'll end up like the others. Dead.

Wyoming: Polly Bartlett: Murderess of Slaughterhouse Gulch

A Town Too Busy to Bury the Dead

In the dust and glitter of the Wyoming gold rush, South Pass exploded into a boomtown. In the 1860s, it was a pulsing artery of gold, whiskey, and hunger—ten thousand souls clawing for fortune, five hotels, seventeen saloons, and too many bodies for anyone to count.

Wayfarers came and went along the Oregon Trail.

But when they vanished, no one noticed.

Or they just shrugged.

It was a place where people disappeared with ease. And that's precisely what the Bartletts were counting on.

The Slaughterhouse Inn

Three miles east of town, nestled in a hollow where the screams wouldn't carry, Jim Bartlett, his daughter Polly, and a shady woman known only as Hattie opened an inn. It was well-placed. Welcoming. A fire always burning. Fresh bread. Smiles.

It was bait. The guests were men alone.

Miners. Brokers. Travelers with gold dust in their boots. They were served stew. They were poured whiskey.

And then, they were fed arsenic.

While Polly smiled and flirted, her father was already digging the grave. Behind the lodge. In the pasture.

Under the hooves of cattle who would trample the earth smooth. Some say she watched them die, the corners of her mouth twitching as the poison took hold.

They say it was never about the gold. It was about control.

About watching the body fail. About enjoying it.

One Mistake Too Few

In April 1868, Polly offered a drink to a man named Edmund Ford. He declined. She insisted. He still refused.

Jim came into the room expecting to see a corpse.

Instead, he found Edmund alive—sober, confused, and now suspicious.

Polly panicked.

She threw him out. She didn't realize he had a brother.

And that brother—Sam Ford—was already on his way.

Polly smiled again. This time, the poison worked.

The Blood in the Pasture

It wasn't until Teddy Fountain, the 23-year-old son of a powerful mine owner, went missing that people began asking questions. Pinkerton detectives came.

The cow pasture was dug up.

Bodies surfaced like rotting roots—limbs bent, teeth still clenched, belt buckles black with decay.

Twenty-two men. Maybe more.

Their bones were crushed from years of hooves walking overhead. But their mouths still opened like they were screaming through the soil.

The End of the Bartletts

Jim Bartlett didn't make it far. Edmund Ford shot him dead when he tried to escape justice.

Polly was found hiding, her skirts soaked from a creek where she'd tried to run. She was jailed.

But she would never stand trial.

Because Otto Kalkhorst, foreman of Teddy Fountain's mine, lifted his rifle, aimed through the jailhouse window, and blew a hole through her skull.

They say no one wept.

No one testified.

And Otto walked away into the dusk.

The Ghost of South Pass

Today, South Pass is quiet. The saloons are dust. The mines are empty. And Polly's inn is long gone.

But visitors still report a woman in black near the edge of the pasture, her hands bloody, her mouth open in a smile that never fades.

And sometimes, late at night, if you stand alone near the graves—

You'll hear a voice behind you whisper:

"Drink?"

Citations

Alabama:
Boyington Oak Tree: 30.686109, -88.051546
The Montgomery Advertiser Montgomery, Alabama Aug 15, 1954
Herald of the Times and Rhode Islander. Sep 02, 1847
findagrave.com/memorial/12693137/charles-r_s_-boyington
turkeystown.com/2025/01/21/uncovering-the-history-of-turkeytown-traditional-location/
Iran Butler: themoonlitroad.com/abels-light-alabama-ghost-story/

Alaska:
nps.gov/klgo/learn/historyculture/jeffsmithsparlor.htm
The Daily Alaskan Skagway, Alaska Jul 11, 1898 Page 4

Arizona:
Brunckow: ghosttowns.com/states/az/brunckowscabin.html

Arkansas:
markberepeterson.com/2021/12/13/urban-legends-haunting-of-the-natural-steps-pulaski-county-arkansas/
The Gurdon light: (2020, Feb 11). thedeadhistory.com/2020/02/11/the-gurdon-light/
Gurdon, AR - Gurdon spook light. roadsideamerica.com/tip/2998

California:
findagrave.com/memorial/53684318/anna_laura-corbin
dreamingcasuallypoetry.blogspot.com/2014/01/what-happened-to-dorothy-waldrop.html
jaimerubiowriter.blogspot.com/2018/03/who-was-anna-corbin-one-of-stories.html

Colorado:
findagrave.com/memorial/140403604
"National Historic Landmarks Program (NHL)".

Connecticut:
lighthousedigest.com/digest/StoryPage.cfm?StoryKey=1452
Norwich bulletin. [volume], Dec 26, 1916, Image 1

Delaware:
Americanwarsus. (2017, Nov 19). Battle of Cooch's bridge | American Revolutionary War. revolutionarywar.us/year-1777/battle-coochs-bridge/

Florida:
staugustinelighthouse.org/2020/03/02/ghost-stories-the-pittee-girls/

Georgia:
militaryghosts.com/phantom-feline-of-fort-mcallister/
train-museum.org/2022/06/23/the-camp-creek-rail-tragedy/

Hawaii:
"Morgan's Corner: The Real Story Behind Hawaii's Most Haunted Road" – Honolulu Magazine honolulumagazine.com